What happened next happened quickly.

Weakened or not, the alien produced a small object—a utility knife, Archer thought—and lifted it upward with the clear intent of disconnecting the oxygen hose that fed from the body of the suit to Hoshi's helmet.

Archer had no way of knowing whether the knife could pierce the strong fiber of the hose, of knowing whether the alien could do her any serious harm. He responded out of pure instinct—drawing the phase pistol from his utility belt, putting his gloved finger on the trigger, aiming and preparing to fire.

But before he could do so, another's phase blast, painfully precise, caught and illumined the alien in the instant before he could bring down the blade.

Archer and Reed reached Hoshi's side at the same time; she sat up, grimaced, and rubbed the back of her skull—in vain, since her helmet kept her from any hands-on contact with the injured area. "I'm fine," she told the captain ruefully. "I tried to say that we were here to help, but the alien . . . He didn't seem sane." She looked up at the crouching Reed. "Thanks for stopping him."

"I didn't shoot," Reed admitted; actually flushed. "I didn't have time."

ENTERPRISE™

SURAK'S SOUL

J. M. DILLARD

Based on *Star Trek*®
created by Gene Roddenberry
Based on *Enterprise*™
created by Rick Berman & Brannon Braga

POCKET BOOKS

New York   London   Toronto   Sydney   Singapore

This book is a work of fiction. Names, characters, places, and incidents are products of the author's imagination or are used fictitiously. Any resemblance to actual events or locales or persons living or dead is entirely coincidental.

An *Original* Publication of POCKET BOOKS

 POCKET BOOKS, a division of Simon & Schuster, Inc. 1230 Avenue of the Americas, New York, NY 10020

 STAR TREK is a Registered Trademark of Paramount Pictures.

This book is published by Pocket Books, a division of Simon & Schuster, Inc., under exclusive license from Paramount Pictures.

ISBN: 0-7434-6280-7

First Pocket Books printing March 2003

10 9 8 7 6 5 4 3 2 1

POCKET and colophon are registered trademarks of Simon & Schuster, Inc.

For information regarding special discounts for bulk purchases, please contact Simon & Schuster Special Sales at 1-800-456-6798 or business@simonandschuster.com

Printed in the U.S.A.

For Dave Stern
for all those opportunities

ACKNOWLEDGMENTS

I am most humbly indebted to editor Margaret Clark for cheerfully giving me the opportunity to write this novel, as well as a great deal of support and information while I was doing so. I'd also like to thank her for remaining blessedly patient when I was a month late in delivering it.

I would be remiss if I failed to mention the two most responsible for helping me in the day-to-day writing of this tome: Hershey and Sweetie Pie. It's a well-known fact that we writers have a tendency to addiction, and I have developed an overwhelming one in recent years. I simply cannot work well without one Labrador stretched out snoring beside me, and another draped over my feet. There are certain disadvantages to this, such as numbness and tingling in the extremities, and then—

well, it *is* avocado season here now, and the dogs have learned to stand on their hindquarters and pick the fruit from the trees. I leave it to the reader's imagination to conjure up the difficulties faced in close quarters with large canines who have eaten heartily of California's fresh produce. The situation may have affected my concentration at times but, I hope, not the quality of storytelling herein.

—Jeanne Dillard
Late July 2002

SURAK'S SOUL

One

Captain's Starlog, Supplemental. While mapping an area of uncharted space, we have encountered a populated planet—which is sending out a beacon that our Universal Translator has garbled. Communications Officer Ensign Hoshi Sato is currently trying to decipher what she can.

JONATHAN ARCHER SAT in his command chair on the bridge of *Enterprise* and stared at the image of the Minshara-class planet on the main viewscreen before him: the larger-than-Earth globe, blue-speckled with large verdant islands rather than continents, rotated lazily.

Frankly, Archer was grateful for the signal, and suspected the rest of his crew was, as well; the

1

process of mapping lifeless planet after lifeless planet had grown tedious, and he was looking forward to some interspecies interaction. He was hoping that this particular planet, which they would have labeled Kappa Xi II, was transmitting its signal in order to welcome interstellar travelers.

He was, in fact, hoping for a distraction. Today was a day that came every year—and every year Archer found a way to remember it, to mark it, and then spent the rest of the day trying to forget so that emotion would not interfere with his efficiency.

That very morning, shortly after he had risen from his bunk—even before he had fed his reproachful-looking beagle, Porthos—he had stepped barefoot over to his tiny closet, removed a picture from the top shelf, and stared at the image for a full minute. It showed Zefram Cochrane, a tall, lean man, all sharp angles, shoulders, and elbows, with a tanned, deeply lined face and a shock of white hair to match his shocking white grin. One of his long, skinny arms was thrown over the shoulders of an equally tall man—this one younger, with dark hair, but with a grin just as wide.

"I'm here, Dad," Archer had said. "I'm really here." The words brought with them both a tightening of his throat and a deep sense of satisfaction; they brought, also, disappointment that his father, Henry Archer, had not lived to see the ship he spent his life building launch.

Today marked the anniversary of Henry Archer's death; and his son Jonathan Archer's life was devoted to fulfilling *Enterprise*'s intended mission—to explore the unknown.

Now, hours later, Archer was seated in his command chair on the *Enterprise* bridge, doing exactly that—and hoping to establish contact with another new race of aliens.

But, as he turned to look expectantly at Hoshi (already under the scrutiny of Ensign Travis Mayweather at helm, Lieutenant Malcolm Reed at tactical, and Sub-Commander T'Pol at the science station), his hope grew fainter. As Hoshi listened and relistened to the message, her dark eyes focused on a far-distant point, her lips resolved themselves into a thinner and thinner line, and the crease between her delicate jet brows deepened.

"Anything?" Archer prompted at last.

"I need more time to do a thorough translation." Hoshi shook her head, then added, "It's not good."

"How so?"

"I'm pretty sure it's a distress call. Some sort of medical emergency. But I can't get any more detailed than that. . . ." She sighed. "From the articulation of the sounds, I'd say the population is humanoid; at least, their lips and tongues and teeth are similar to ours."

Archer considered this for no more than a matter of seconds, then turned to T'Pol, lithe and spare in her formfitting, no-frills Vulcan uniform, and an equally understated and efficient cap of nape-length ash hair. "What's the atmosphere down there?"

The Vulcan swiveled gracefully to her station, then looked back at the captain, her expression and tone impassive, despite the news she conveyed. "Breathable. However . . ." Her gaze became pointed. "I detect very few life-forms."

It took Archer no more than an instant to make a decision. Regardless of the number of survivors, *Enterprise* was present, capable of assistance, and therefore obligated to intervene. An entire species, perhaps, was at risk of annihilation. He pressed the intercom. "Archer to sickbay."

"Phlox here."

Keeping his gaze fixed on the worried Hoshi, Archer said, "Doctor, we have an unknown medical emergency down on the planet's surface; the population is probably humanoid. Bring whatever you need to the shuttlepod launch bay. Archer out."

He stood. "Hoshi, I'll need you to translate what you can. T'Pol, Reed . . ." He gestured with his chin, and together the four of them headed for the bridge doors. "Mr. Mayweather, you have the conn."

* * *

The flight down to Kappa Xi II's surface was pleasant; Archer was privately cheered by Hoshi's attitude toward it. She had made up her mind to learn to enjoy such expeditions, and peered through the small viewscreen at the looming image of large emerald islands adrift in a vast turquoise sea—a far different distribution of land to water than on Earth.

"Gorgeous," Archer murmured, half to himself, as he piloted the shuttlepod closer to one of the larger islands, their destination.

"Yes," Hoshi echoed, while Phlox made an enthusiastic noise. "Too bad they're having an emergency. This looks like it would be a beautiful place for shore leave. . . ."

"Quite the tropical paradise," Reed added.

Archer smiled faintly to himself, remembering the pleasant times he had spent on the island of Kauai. "Just don't expect to be welcomed with garlands of flowers, Lieutenant."

"It *is* rather Earthlike," T'Pol commented neutrally from the jump seat, which made the captain consider that a blue-green planet might seem inviting to humans, but perhaps to Vulcan eyes, a red desert planet would be more aesthetically pleasing.

Still, the ride down through the atmosphere to the coastline of the island was breathtaking; the water closer to the shore was celery-colored and so clear that even from a distance brightly colored creatures could be seen swimming beneath the surface. The sand was pure white, reminding Archer of a Florida beach he'd once visited; at the meeting of water and shore, long-legged birds raced to pluck buried meals from the wet sand before waves rolled in again. *Too bad Trip isn't here to see this.* Trip Tucker, *Enterprise*'s chief engineer and the captain's best friend, had spent years scuba-diving in the Keys.

Archer brought the shuttlepod to a smooth landing at its destination, a large paved strip closest to the largest cluster of remaining life-forms. He had wondered whether this large paved area was used strictly for planetbound air travel—but a glance at his surroundings made it clear that this culture, if not used to extraterrestrial contact, was probably capable of spaceflight. In a nearby hangar, a number of sophisticated vessels rested; Archer eyed them covetously as he brought the shuttlepod to a halt, wishing there were time to inspect them. Instead, he pushed the hatch controls open, and followed his away team out onto the landing strip, adjacent to the coastline.

Once outside, the first thing Archer noticed was the sun: the sun, shining bright in a cloudless Earth-blue sky, the sun reflecting off the nearby diamond-white sand, off the dappled water, off tall, spiraling buildings that shone like mother of pearl, reflecting pale green, turquoise, and rose. Tall trees, their great blue-green leaves draping down like weeping willows, rustled in a light breeze.

"An island paradise." Archer sighed. The landing party had dressed in their copper-bronze colored spacesuits on Dr. Phlox's insistence. Had the captain been alone, he would have risked exposure and relied on the decontam procedures on board *Enterprise* just for the chance to feel the sun and wind against his bare skin. The notion of breathing in a lungful of sea air was enticing. Besides, the suits, with their domed helmets, might make them look rather outlandish to any species unused to regular extraterrestrial contact. But he respected Phlox's opinion, and where his crew members were concerned, he would take all precautions. Reed had insisted on them arming themselves with phase pistols. Medical emergency or not, it was impossible to predict exactly what they might encounter.

"Beautiful," Reed breathed.

"Ambient temperature twenty-five degrees Celsius," T'Pol announced clinically, her gaze on her scanner. "Life-forms . . ." She paused, then pointed in the direction of the spiraling buildings. "In that direction, Captain. Very few, and very faint."

"Let's move," Archer said, all appreciation for his surroundings dismissed. He led the group at a rapid pace, slowing only when Hoshi cried out behind him.

"Captain!"

He turned and followed his communication officer's gaze. Peeking out from the profile of one of the silver ships was a hand. Not a human hand—this one was six-fingered, curled in a limp half fist, the skin a deep greenish bronze.

Archer arrived at the humanoid's side first, closely followed by Phlox. In the open hatch of the shuttle-sized ship, a male had fallen backward, so that his torso lay faceup on the stone-and-shale landing strip, his legs on the deck of his vessel. Clearly, he'd been stricken as he attempted to leave . . . fleeing, perhaps, whatever had decimated his people. His complexion was deep bronze, his scalp and ridged brow were entirely hairless; the cartilage of his nose terminated in a sharp, triangular tip, framed by large diagonal slits for nostrils. He stared up at the cloudless sky with almost perfectly round, dark eyes, dulled by death. His expression was entirely neutral, his lipless mouth open to reveal a hard dental ridge mostly covered by pale gums. The hands that fell so limply from his flailed arms were slightly webbed, suggesting that his people had evolved from the sea that covered most of their planet. His clearly muscular body was draped in a soft white, semi-sheer toga with full, winglike arms that made Archer think of the snow angels he'd made as a child.

Whatever had taken his life, Archer decided,

had not inspired fear in him, even if he was running away. He got the impression that the man had sagged gently to the ground, as if he had simply no longer been able to hold himself erect.

Phlox crouched over the body and scanned it briefly. He glanced up at Archer and said softly, sadly, "Already dead, I fear. Very recently."

Archer gave a single regretful nod.

The doctor studied his readouts, then gently touched the dead humanoid, examining the eyes, nose, mouth, and torso. "I'm not detecting anything microbial in his system. . . ." He looked up at Archer, his features furrowed with puzzlement. "In fact, I can't really tell you what he died of. My first guess is that these readings are normal for him . . . but it would help if I had a healthy member of his race for comparison."

Reed drew his phase pistol and disappeared into the ship for several seconds, then emerged again, his expression one of awe. "No other bodies, sir. But these people are definitely capable of spaceflight. I know Commander Tucker would love to take one of these apart—we could learn a thing or two. . . ."

"Later, Lieutenant," Archer answered shortly.

"Captain," T'Pol said quietly. Archer took a step toward her and glanced over her shoulder at her scanner. "Chances of finding such a being are becoming slimmer. Since we have left *Enterprise*, many more life-forms have died. I'm now reading only eleven on this island. The signals are growing increasingly faint."

"Let's move," Archer said again, gazing down at the dead man, feeling oddly reluctant to leave him without some acknowledgment, some rite to mark his passage. But as the captain turned to face the alien city, he realized the necessity for speed—else they would be needing a memorial to mark the passage of an entire civilization.

As the quintet strode quickly over a shale-and-sand street toward the building T'Pol indicated, they were met by grisly sights: pedestrians fallen as they walked, in different stages of decomposition under the bright sun. Airborne vehicles carrying single passengers, sometimes pairs, had dropped from the sky, leaving mangled wreckage and toga-draped corpses—some on the ground, others caught in the swaying trees, or on shrubs, or lying atop a bier of brightly colored flowers. At one point, they passed a body being attended to by a carrion bird; Hoshi briefly closed her eyes, but moved stalwartly onward. Once again, Archer got the impression that the victims had surrendered easily and unexpectedly to death, in the midst of going about their lives.

He was finally glad for the awkward suit, with its self-contained atmosphere; the smell of decay must have been overwhelming. He thought of Earth's past plagues, and the terror that must have been felt by the survivors. During the Black Plague in medieval Europe, there had been so many dead, the living could not bury them all; a similar thing had happened during the plagues that swept mankind after the third World War. And it had happened to these poor people, in the midst of their beautiful paradise.

Death came too swiftly sometimes, Archer decided. He was an enormously lucky man; he had lived long enough to be able to do exactly what he wanted to do with his life. . . . *Yeah, and Dad lived long enough, but was denied the one dream he had.* . . . Archer forced himself to ignore the last thought. At least his father had had the time to create something of real value. But these people—they were stricken in midstride, without warning. Had they had the chance to achieve their goals?

He maintained silence, forcing himself to concentrate on the waiting survivors who needed their help; only Hoshi spoke, uttering a single plaintive remark.

"I only hope there's someone left for me to try to talk to."

No one replied—not even Phlox. The streets were still, quiet save for the sound of wind rustling through long leaves, and the cries of seabirds.

The landing party soon reached their destination: a building with shimmering, nacreous walls that coiled delicately skyward. Large windows overlooked the sea.

"Like a nautilus shell," Malcolm Reed said as he stared upward, his tone hushed and reverent in honor of the dead. His chiseled, somewhat hawkish features—so distinctly British, Archer decided—stood in profile against the cyan sky.

Yet the building's beauty belied the horror that waited inside. As Archer and his group entered, they were met by an eerie sight. In a large sun-filled room with a view of the sparkling beach, some sixty or seventy bronze-skinned people sat cross-legged on the padded floor—some fallen forward, faces pressed to the ground, others fallen back against the walls. All wore the same gentle, relaxed expression of the first casualty the away team had encountered.

Hoshi failed to entirely surpress a gasp; even T'Pol's eyes, behind her visor, flickered for an instant as she steadied herself to do a quick scan.

"Survivors this way," she said softly, pointing down a gleaming corridor.

Phlox turned his broad body directly toward the sight, absorbing it fully. "A shame," he said. "A peaceful people, able to build such a marvelous city . . . and now, most of them gone."

Archer put a hand on his shoulder. "Let's go find those survivors, Doctor."

Phlox turned, shaking his head as he moved alongside the captain. "You read of such things happening in history, but you never wish to see such a thing yourself. . . ."

Reed remained altogether silent, keeping his pistol drawn.

T'Pol led the way down the corridor; they passed several rooms, all of them filled with exotic-looking beds made of a shimmering gelatinous material that caught Archer's eye, but there was no time left to stop and inspect them. Atop each one lay one, sometimes two, bodies; after a time, Archer stopped looking.

A moment or two later, the Vulcan said, with the faintest hint of something suspiciously akin to excitement, "Survivor, Captain. This room . . ."

They entered; Archer moved aside so Phlox could attend to his patient at once. Eagerly, Hoshi moved beside the doctor, in case she was needed to communicate. The alien—this one, judging by her more delicate features and smaller size, female—was partially encased in a bed composed of a blue-green gelatinous substance suspended in the air.

Phlox scanned the woman, then exchanged a knowing glance with T'Pol.

"What?" Archer demanded of the two.

Both paused, then Phlox spoke. "This woman has just died."

"Another survivor," T'Pol added swiftly. "Aproximately zero-point-one-seven kilometers down the corridor. . . ."

Archer made his way into the hallway at a speed just shy of a full run; T'Pol outpaced him, leading the way as Reed, then Hoshi and Phlox followed. Two doors down, the Vulcan entered what appeared to be a large, fully equipped medical laboratory. Several suspended beds lay empty, but on the one nearest the entrance lay a patient—half covered by the body of another alien, who had apparently been standing over the bed when he was stricken.

The bed itself was glowing, phosphorescent, slightly pulsating; Archer could feel the warmth it emanated as he helped Reed lift the body of the male off the smaller, prone patient.

"Poor sod," Reed murmured. "Probably died trying to save her."

As the *Enterprise* officers gently eased the male to the floor, Phlox leaned forward and ran a scanner over his chest. "Dead." The doctor turned and swiftly made his way over to the reclining patient—a female. "But she's alive!" His tone was one of pure triumph; as he ran his medical scanner over her, he reported, "But weakening with each second. Electrolyte readings differ from those found in the dead victims. . . ." He opened his medical case and prepared an injection. As he administered it, the blue-green bed flickered, then began to brighten, shot through with glowing phosphorescent veins.

"A nutrient bed," Phlox murmured, while he attended the woman. "Probably to counteract the weakness. I'll wager it's to help stabilize her electrolytes. . . ." He trailed off, absorbed in his work.

Archer, meantime, could not help noticing the expression on the male victim's face; of all the dead the captain had seen, only this man's countenance was not peaceful. Indeed, his features were contorted with what a human would call outrage, even—*Am I reading my own cultural cues into this?* Archer wondered—recognition, as if he had recognized the cause of his own death and been incensed by it.

"Anyone else still with us?" Archer asked softly of T'Pol, who was busily scanning for readings.

Her eyes narrowed. "No survivors in this building. But roughly zero-point-five-four kilometers northeast, there's one fairly strong signal left."

"And the others?"

Her gaze grew pointed. "There *are* no others, Captain. Not on this island. Not anymore."

You said there were eleven, Archer almost said, then realized the futility of challenging the accuracy of T'Pol's reading. In the moments since they'd arrived on the island, nine of those survivors had died.

He made a decision. "Stay with her," he told Phlox, who was busily bent over the surviving female. "Reed, Hoshi, you come with us. T'Pol and I are going to go find the last survivor and bring him back here; Hoshi, we might need your help communicating after all."

"Fascinating medical apparatus," Phlox murmured, his gaze fixed on his patient, but Hoshi nodded in acknowledgment.

"Aye, sir."

Despite the fact that they were in the midst of a city, T'Pol led the captain, Reed, and Hoshi into what seemed to be a livestock facility, where smooth-skinned quadrupeds, looking rather like overfed manatees on legs, lay motionless, perished in their separate stalls. Troughs of untouched grain and water lay in each pen. Overhead were storage lofts holding containers of what appeared to be feed.

There was an endearing ugliness about the creatures, and the fact that the pens were clean and in fact padded for comfort made Archer somehow sadder than he'd been before. It was hard enough to witness the death of a sentient being, who was aware of his own mortality; but there was a special poignancy about the demise of a less intelligent creature who trusted others for its care. The image of his beagle, Porthos, flashed in Archer's mind.

A single glance at Hoshi's heartbroken expression made Archer look away. Reed managed not to react, but his brow remained deeply furrowed, and one corner of his mouth was pulled taut with horrified pity.

"All recently deceased," T'Pol said clinically, passing them with no more than a cursory glance.

Archer hardened his attitude and followed the Vulcan closely, focusing on the task at hand. "So the plague—or whatever's caused this—has affected their animals, too."

"With the exception of some of the smaller fauna," T'Pol remarked—then came to an abrupt halt, lifting a hand for silence.

Archer and Reed stopped behind her; Hoshi, last in line, bumped into them both.

The two women heard the noise first—of course, given T'Pol's acute Vulcan hearing and Hoshi's amazing exolinguistic ears. Both looked upward, expectantly, at the same area in one of the lofts.

Hoshi uttered a few tentative sounds in the aliens' tongue, her voice a little higher-pitched than normal—whether from proper pronunciation or fear, Archer could not tell. A greeting, perhaps, or an offer to help.

What happened next happened so quickly that for Archer, it all blurred together.

An alien face—deep bronze, with round, luminous, *living* eyes—appeared overhead amid the stacks of feed containers. A male, given the size and bulk; the low-ceilinged loft forced him to crawl on hands and knees. He scrambled to the edge of the loft and looked down at the landing party.

Glowered, actually, but Archer's observation was overwhelmed by the jubilant thought: *Alive! He's alive and strong enough to talk!*

And, indeed, the alien opened his lipless mouth and let go a sound. An unarticulated sound, more like a low growl that began deep in his broad chest and left his throat as a shriek . . .

. . . As he came springing down, arms outstretched, one webbed, many-fingered hand grasping, its target Hoshi's throat.

The communications officer screamed as the alien leapt atop her, knocking her down hard—so hard that, despite the protection provided by her helmet, Archer could hear her skull thud.

Weakened or not, the alien produced a small object—a utility knife, Archer thought—and lifted it upward with the clear intent of disconnecting the oxygen hose that fed from the body of the suit to Hoshi's helmet.

Archer had no way of knowing whether the knife could pierce the strong fiber of the hose, of knowing whether the alien could do her any serious harm. He responded out of pure instinct—drawing the phase pistol from his utility belt, putting his gloved finger on the trigger, aiming and preparing to fire.

But before he could do so, another's phase blast, painfully precise, caught and illumined the alien in the instant before he could bring down the blade.

He shuddered, hesitated in the air a half second, then fell heavily to one side, allowing the terrified Hoshi to scrabble backward, crablike, on her arms and legs.

Archer and Reed reached Hoshi's side at the same time; she sat up, grimaced, and rubbed the back of her skull—in vain, since her helmet kept her from any hands-on contact with the injured area. "I'm fine," she told the captain ruefully. "I tried to say that we were here to help, but the alien . . . he didn't seem sane." She looked up at the crouching Reed. "Thanks for stopping him."

"I didn't shoot," Reed admitted, awkwardly; he actually flushed. "I didn't have time."

The three humans glanced over at the fallen man, then at T'Pol, who bent over him with her scanner. Her phase pistol was already reholstered, her air already that of the impassive scientist; yet there was the subtlest catch in her tone as she looked up at Archer and announced:

"Dead, Captain. Given his weakened state, my stun blast killed him."

Two

THE SILENCE on the shuttlepod ride back to the ship was palpable.

The team had failed abysmally in its mission: The woman in Phlox's care had died despite all of the doctor's desperate ministrations; and every attempt by the quartet of Archer, Reed, T'Pol, and Hoshi to locate and rescue other survivors had ended in their discovering a recently deceased individual. Eventually, T'Pol's scanner no longer registered any life-forms other than birds and insects. Standing beneath Kappa Xi II's glorious bright sun, Archer had been forced to admit defeat. An entire civilization was dead, and nothing they had done had stopped it.

The thought flashed in Archer's mind: *I'm sorry, Dad. We did what we could.*

Phlox had begged for permission to bring two of the bodies aboard: those of the man and the woman who had been found together in the medical facility while the woman was still alive. Archer had reluctantly agreed, knowing Phlox would maintain them under the strictest quarantine. The landing party had waited while specially designed containers were beamed down, and Phlox followed careful procedures to place the bodies inside. The sealed containers would go through decontam along with everyone else. In addition, Phlox collected tissue and blood samples from other victims for comparison.

Yet even if Phlox and his techs managed to solve the mystery of what had killed those on the island planet, Archer wondered what good it would serve—then mentally drew himself up short. His expression had become as grim as the doctor's, as Hoshi's.

Giving in to guilt is as bad as feeling sorry for yourself. You couldn't help. Leave it at that. But finding out what caused this tragedy might help others, including those on your own ship.

"It's not your fault, you know," Hoshi said suddenly behind him, from the passenger's seat; he half turned his head to glance back at her—and realized that Hoshi was speaking not to him but to T'Pol.

"I do not understand," the Vulcan replied evenly, without taking her eyes off the copilot

21

controls. Of the landing party, only T'Pol had maintained a neutral expression, and had not exuded a sense of dismalness.

"That the man died back there. When you protected me."

"Ah." T'Pol's expression and tone were cool, uninflected. "You are referring to my shooting the alien and his subsequent death."

Archer had to admit to himself that he was surprised by the fact that it had been T'Pol, and not Reed, who had reacted more swiftly with the phase pistol. *Of course, just because she's a pacifist doesn't mean she's not a crack shot.* Reed listened to the two women and averted his gaze, paying undue attention to the scene outside the craft; Archer assumed that the lieutenant was still somewhat embarrassed that he hadn't been the one to react quickly.

"Yes," Hoshi said earnestly. "I just wanted you to know that it wasn't your fault. You may have saved my life, and you had no way of knowing that a stun blast would kill him. You shouldn't feel bad about it."

Archer felt for an instant like a self-absorbed heel. Here he'd been depressed about his own inability to help—yet how must the peaceable Vulcan feel, knowing that she was responsible for the death of one of the last survivors?

T'Pol's eyes flickered briefly; watching through the ports as *Enterprise* loomed closer, she responded: "I still do not understand your need to assign or not assign fault. An event happened. It was simple cause and effect. I perceived the alien as attacking you, and responded by taking a particular action. I am incapable of, as you put it, 'feeling bad' about it."

Hoshi's expression soured; she folded her arms over her chest and said shortly, "Fine. I just didn't want you to feel guilty."

"Guilt is a human emotion," T'Pol said, with something suspiciously like pride. *So*, thought Archer, *it must be nice to live without any self-doubt. And here I'd been worried about her reaction to the alien's death. . . .*

"Fine," Hoshi repeated, and said no more until they arrived at the ship.

In the decontamination chamber aboard *Enterprise*, Malcolm Reed found himself presented with a situation straight from his fondest dreams.

Stripped down to her underwear, the long-limbed T'Pol, proffered him a large jar of iridescent decontamination gel. "Lieutenant," she said, in her cool, low voice, "if you would be so kind."

Reed only hoped he wasn't staring. He'd done his best to maintain the ultimate decorum around all female members of *Enterprise*, for he was military first, and male second, and frowned on even the merest hint of fraternization.

As for T'Pol, Reed had been reluctant to admit,

even to himself, his attraction to her. Only Trip Tucker knew, and then only because Reed had confessed his attraction during an incontrovertibly drunken moment.

He'd always considered Vulcan women very attractive—the exotic upsweep of their ears, perhaps, or more likely the fact that they were unapproachable, untouchable, unknowable, taboo. . . .

But he had come to know T'Pol, at least, just a bit. She was everything a woman ought to be—graceful in her every movement, incredibly intelligent, courteous, refined, dignified . . . *Come to think of it,* Reed told himself honestly, *everything that I wish I could be all the time. Except female.*

And she was now standing in front of him waiting for Reed, to smear her back with the gel—after which, she would do the same for him.

Nearby, Phlox was finishing up the captain's back for him, while Hoshi sat patiently, already thoroughly coated.

Reed kept his features composed in a serious near-scowl, and accepted the container of gel with a curt, professional nod. Phlox and the captain were busily talking, and Hoshi was listening to them; the distraction presented Reed and T'Pol with something close to a private moment.

Reed had been somewhat concerned by two things—first, that he had been outgunned by T'Pol, since *he* was the tactical officer, after all. It wasn't easy for him to accept that, since he was a mere human, any Vulcan would always have a much faster reaction time, no matter how many years Reed spent practicing with his phase pistol. Yet he knew he had to accept such a fact with grace; there was enough human/Vulcan prejudice in the galaxy as it was, and he felt it his duty to try to overcome any such prejudice he found within himself.

Thus, he felt it was important for him to maintain as friendly a relationship with T'Pol as possible—*for the sake of human-Vulcan relations*, he told himself quite seriously.

Second, he was concerned about T'Pol's own reaction to inadvertently killing the alien. Hoshi's comments in the shuttlepod, followed by T'Pol's more-than-usual stiff behavior afterward, made Reed worry that perhaps the Vulcan indeed felt guilt about the situation.

And so, as T'Pol turned her back to him, and Reed smoothed the first bit of phosphorescent gel over the curve of her shoulder, he remarked, "Hoshi was right, you know."

"About what?" T'Pol's tone appeared entirely flat, indifferent.

"There was nothing you could have done about killing that alien. I mean, he was bound to die one way or another."

T'Pol did not respond. Reed slicked down the other shoulder, then began to move toward the small of her back. She was really quite amazingly muscular, though she did not appear so—her muscles were firmer than a human male's, yet her skin was so much softer. . . .

Reed forced his thoughts to the issue at hand. T'Pol's lack of response increased his sense of awkwardness. "What I'm trying to say is . . . you mustn't feel responsible for killing off an entire race. Just because he was the last . . . We probably wouldn't have learned that much from him, even if Hoshi had had the chance to communicate with him."

Reed trailed off, realizing he was simply digging the hole deeper. He began rubbing the gel on more vigorously. T'Pol's posture stiffened and she said, "Lieutenant."

Reed continued his work, with such intensity that he began to huff a bit. "I'm not accusing you of guilt, mind you, I just want you to know that you don't bear the responsibility . . ."

"*Lieutenant,*" T'Pol said, and Reed suddenly realized, that he had been rubbing in the gel with too much vigor. "I do not believe you are required to penetrate the epidermal layer."

Heat rushed to Reed's face; without another word, he handed over the container of gel, then averted his eyes as T'Pol administered the decontaminant to the rest of her body. He sat down on the nearby bench, stricken into silence.

T'Pol dipped her hand into the container of gel, and said, "Lieutenant. Your back . . . ?"

At first he did not understand, and then he realized that she was working to return the favor. He turned his back toward her and replied, in what he hoped was an indifferent tone, "Of course . . ."

Once T'Pol had finished, she straightened. "Lieutenant . . . I appreciate your concern."

"You do?" Reed turned toward her in surprise.

T'Pol cleared her throat delicately. "However, it is misplaced and inappropriate. You are engaging in what your psychotherapists would call 'mind reading'—you are ascribing your own emotional reactions and thoughts to me, just as Hoshi did."

"Oh."

"I would appreciate it if you could resist doing so."

"I'll . . . do my best to resist," Reed said.

In her small, spartan quarters that evening, T'Pol sat cross-legged on the deck, spine perfectly straight as she leaned forward and lit her meditation candle.

It was still early in the evening, but she had begun her meditation ritual ahead of schedule in order to settle her thoughts. Captain Archer had rejected her request to work a second shift that night in the medical lab alongside Dr. Phlox. There was no hurry now, he'd said grimly; he'd prefer fresh minds in the morning to tackle the problem. T'Pol could take over on the science end when Phlox needed rest. He'd even ordered

Hoshi—who was responsible for deciphering a great deal of audio and video records brought from the surface, and eager to get to work—to take a night's rest first.

T'Pol had felt oddly troubled since shooting the alien down on the planet's surface; troubled, indeed, to the point where she had come close to saying something to the captain as they had all been sitting, smeared with gel, in the decontamination chamber. Yet she had not known precisely what she had wanted to say.

She knew only that she should not have shot the alien; her action had been a mistake, one that led to his untimely death. In the context of the planetary catastrophe, that one premature death had very broad and disturbing implications. The mystery of his peers' deaths might now never be solved.

T'Pol settled back into the prescribed position, let go a deep breath, closed her eyes, and forced all thoughts from her.

For an instant, no more, there was silence, and darkness.

And then the image of the dead alien, lying at her feet, rose unbidden. Why had she not considered the possible consequences of her action before she fired? Admittedly, she had acted not on intelligence but on pure impulse. Had her time among humans begun to affect her so deeply?

She rejected the latter question as soon as it

arose. She had already told Hoshi that guilt was illogical; so, too, was blame, and she would not lay the responsibility for her own actions at the humans' feet.

Once again, T'Pol struggled to quiet her mind.

The image of the dead alien resurfaced once more; she remembered the instruction of her meditation teacher. *If an image will not leave you, simply focus on it. See where it leads; in doing so, you will clear the obstruction it represents. Only then will you be able to successfully meditate.*

T'Pol let go a deep, closemouthed sigh, drew in a fresh breath, and this time studied the image closely when it presented itself.

And at once, she was no longer a woman sitting on the deck of a starship hurtling at subwarp speed in orbit about an unknown planet, but a girl, kneeling in the hot red sand of a Vulcan garden.

Before her, a desert succulent, a large *kal'ta* plant, lay uprooted and limp beneath the relentless sun, its deep violet leaves, edged with iridescent blue, partially eaten away. The plant had grown for years in the garden, well before T'Pol's birth; vast and venerable, it had been her father's favorite, grown from a cutting handed down in the family for unbroken generations.

Now it lay destroyed; and as young T'Pol studied the damage, aghast (yet even at the age of five years being trained enough to control the outward expression of what she felt), she heard her mother's calm voice addressing her father just inside the house.

"A *ch'kariya*, no doubt. I will purchase a trap for it, and contact your father for another cutting from his *kal'ta.*"

A *ch'kariya:* a burrowing mammal that relied on the roots of plants for water and nourishment. T'Pol had never seen one, and when she heard her mother's word, an idea struck the young scientist: she would construct a trap herself, immediately, from materials already in the family home, and capture the creature for observation. This would do two positive things: please her parents, and further her knowledge of Vulcan zoology.

T'Pol immediately constructed a simple trap, no more than a tranparent box with one side that was rigged to slide closed when the animal entered. As bait, she left a small portion of the *kal'ta* plant with its roots attached.

By sunset, her plan bore fruit: inside the box she found a long, slender quadruped, pale-skinned with sparse hair, so small she could hold it in her hands. Its tiny eyes were squinted shut, blinded even by the waning light of dusk.

She said nothing to her parents, but carried it to her room in secrecy. That night, for many hours, she observed the creature, who, once it decided it was in no imminent danger, wolfed down the bit of plant and root. After a time, it grew sluggish, and apparently went to sleep; pleased that she had gained quite a bit of independent information, T'Pol did the same.

When she woke the following morning, the animal was motionless and would not be roused, despite her prodding. Alarmed, she took it at once to her parents, who were seated on the stone meditation bench in the garden. At the sound of her faster-than-normal steps, they both opened their eyes and gazed serenely at her, and at the boxed creature in her hands.

Her mother, jet-haired and black-eyed, waited calmly for her daughter to speak. She had the darker coloration typical of most Vulcans, which T'Pol envied and secretly thought was more beautiful; the girl had inherited her father's lighter eyes, skin, and hair.

"I trapped the *ch'kariya*," T'Pol said, fighting to keep the childish anxiety from her voice. "I studied it last night and meant to free it in the desert today. But there's something wrong with it."

Her father took the box from her, opened it, and reached in to touch the creature. After a second of examination, he confirmed T'Pol's suspicion. "It is dead."

T'Pol bowed her head in utter shame and dismay. Had she been any younger, any less trained in emotional control, she would have wept. She had committed the most heinous crime possible in Vulcan culture: she had killed needlessly.

"I suspect it starved to death," her father continued, his pale eyes bearing a hint of reproach. *"Ch'kariyas* require a great deal of sustenance because of their high metabolic rate. Did you supply it with a large amount of vegetation?"

Miserable, T'Pol shook her head.

"We are Vulcans," her mother said softly. "We are the most intelligent species on this planet, and thus far, more intelligent than any other species we have encountered in space. Physically, we are stronger than most other creatures we have encountered; given the combination, we have an extremely great potential to cause harm.

"Thus, we also have the greatest responsibility to utilize our intelligence and to control our impulses.

"You see how easy it is to accidentally harm, even to kill. This is why we study the teachings of Surak, that we might avoid our natural impulse to wreak violence. We struggle daily, we meditate, we utilize our intelligence to its maximum, all in order to master that impulse.

"Now you must learn how to take great care in your every action to avoid causing harm. Intelligence is worthless if it is not backed by compassion."

"I will never forget what my carelessness has caused," young T'Pol said, lifting her chin to at last directly meet her mother's steady gaze. "I promise you that I will never again cause the death of any creature."

Her father spoke at last. "Over the course of your life, you may find, daughter, that yours is not such an easy promise to keep."

A new image surfaced in T'Pol's memory, that of the highly esteemed Vulcan master Sklar, who had come to her city to lecture students. In this case, he had agreed, for the first time in his two centuries of teaching, to lecture the intermediate students as well as the advanced. T'Pol, now aged ten, had recently moved up into the intermediate category, and was thrilled at the opportunity.

She had sat some distance in the city's vast auditorium from the speaker, who used no technical enhancement to be heard, but relied solely upon his strong, resonant voice. T'Pol had no difficulty hearing every word; she was in fact mesmerized by each one, by the grace and serenity that emanated from the elder's posture and expression, by the way the filtered sunlight glinted off his purely white hair. Here was one who had attained the blissful state of *Kolinahr*, nonemotion; here was one whose life was fully devoted to the pursuit of peace.

He spoke at first of Surak, the revered bringer of peace to the planet Vulcan, the one whose philosophy had stopped the raging wars, had transformed the culture from one devoted to violence and bloodshed to one devoted to compassion, to unity, to logic.

"Surak's earliest teachings spoke of complete nonviolence, a truly noble concept. He carried no weapon, he offered no defense—yet he brought down the fiercest warlords Vulcan has ever seen with his words.

"We are Surak's heirs. But we must never let ourselves grow complacent or arrogant, thinking that we are the only ones in the universe capable of such a great philosophy. Others have come to similar conclusions. Can anyone here think of another culture besides ours where one arose to teach peace?"

Stillness in the auditorium. No one replied, so Sklar gave the single-word answer.

"Earth."

Had it been humans sitting in the audience, everyone would have gasped. As it was, the stillness grew heavier: T'Pol leaned forward ever so slightly, awaiting the explanation for such an unexpected answer.

"His name was Mohandas K. Gandhi, and he lived on twentieth-century Earth, in an area called India at the time. He was a Hindu, and believed in the principle of *ahimsa*, a Sanskrit term for the concept of total nonviolence toward every living being. Following *ahimsa*, Gandhi-ji, as he became known, convinced the Indians to give up their internal fighting and unite against a common foe: Great Britain, which had invaded their country and instituted a government which treated the Indians as inferior.

"His strategy was successful: the humans used nonviolent protest and, without killing, without war, shamed Britain into leaving their country. Gandhi-ji had a great victory.

"In the end, however, he was killed by one of his own, who was angered by the thought of cultural unity. His philosophy of peace failed to transform Earth; humans are still haunted by the specter of violence. Many terrible wars followed the death of Gandhi-ji, and in fact, India itself was divided into factions—not without more bloodshed."

Sklar paused; had T'Pol believed him capable of emotion, she might have said that slyness flickered over his features.

"Here is the question I pose to you today, not in hope of a verbal answer, but in hope of inciting thought. It remains a matter of debate, even among those of us in the *Kolinahr* community." Again he paused. "Should Gandhi-ji have defended himself from violence? Should he have carried a weapon in order to protect himself—not out of pure self-interest, but in order to protect his peace movement? Or was he right to let himself be destroyed?"

No one answered, but a slight rustling could be heard in the audience, as T'Pol and her peers glanced uneasily at each other, trying to gauge the general consensus. Finally, a young male rose and said, "With your permission, Sklar."

The elder nodded.

"Surak bore no weapon, yet he managed to convince other Vulcans of the time to follow his philosophy. In fact, he took many risks by approaching notorious warlords."

"Vulcans have a renowned capacity for self-discipline," Sklar replied, "which perhaps allowed Surak's movement to spread more easily, without Vulcans relapsing into violence. Surak also had tested many methods on himself for years before he began sharing his philosophy— methods for reducing our violent tendencies which we still employ today." He motioned for the child to sit down, then addressed the crowd. "In fact, our own government employs protective devices as deterrents . . . devices which could even be called 'weapons.' We do not venture into space without weapons, in order to protect ourselves in case we encounter more violent species. Yet the chance exists that those weapons might be accidentally misused. Are we still justified in bearing them?"

T'Pol stood up. "With your permission, Sklar."

Again, a nod.

"We have the right to defend ourselves," she said, "against species who would bring about our destruction."

"So, hypothetically," Sklar responded, "if a warlike alien species threatened to destroy our planet, our entire civilization, we would be justified in protecting ourselves."

"Most definitely," T'Pol answered confidently.

"Even if it means destroying the alien species," Sklar finished. His words had the intonation of a sentence, but it was most definitely a question, a challenge. *Regarding violence, where do we draw the line? How deeply must we commit ourselves to peace if it is truly to affect the universe around us?*

T'Pol stood for a few seconds longer, casting about for a reply, and then she sat down. For the rest of the lecture, she remained silent.

At last, as she opened her eyes and stared at the glowing flame on the candle in front of her, the adult T'Pol's mind was at rest. She drew in another breath and prepared herself for the ritual of meditation. As she did, she repeated silently to herself a verse from the teachings of Surak:

The breath we draw in and release is peace. The thoughts in our minds are peace. Our body, our limbs are peace. Our spirit, our essence is peace. . . .

And as she released herself into the nothingness that was meditation, T'Pol herself was finally at peace. She had made her decision concerning the alien's death; she knew what to do to make amends.

* * *

Yet another memory came to her, this one far more painful to the other two: the recollection of herself some seventeen years before, running through the steamy, tropical jungle on Risa, pursuing Menos and his cohort, Jossen. Both were Vulcans who had been surgically altered in order to infiltrate a group of smugglers from the planet Agaron—but they had chosen to reject their Vulcan upbringing and had instead joined the very group they had been sent to disband.

And T'Pol had been chosen by the Vulcan government to bring them back.

Flash of an image, vivid, emotionally disturbing: Jossen, fallen to the ground, reaching for his weapon . . .

T'Pol had fired, instinctively . . .

And in a brilliant, blazing millisecond had killed.

She had been very young then; the fact had left her devastated. Unable to fulfill her duties, she had sought help at the Sanctuary at P'Jem, where she had undergone the ancient Vulcan ritual of *Fullara*, which eradicated both traumatic memories and all attendant emotions.

But the ritual, ultimately, had failed; her memory had returned.

It returned full force now, as did the promise she had made to herself—that she would never

again allow herself to take a life, even accidentally.

Now, she had failed.

In the captain's dining room, Hoshi stared dis-
mally down at her plate of stir-fried tofu atop a
bed of greens. She had yet to take a bite, although Archer was three-quarters of the way
through his meal, and Trip had already finished.
As for Malcolm, the Englishman had eaten perhaps half of his spaghetti, and was obsessively
organizing the rest of it into neatly coiled
mounds on his plate.

The captain had insisted on Malcolm and
Hoshi joining him for dinner; he was especially
concerned about the landing party's reaction—especially Hoshi's—to the sad scenario down on the
planet's surface. In decontam, Hoshi had folded
her arms tightly about her, lips taut, and said not
a word to anyone, although Archer had tried a
couple of times to gently engage her in conversation. T'Pol had been as emotionless as ever, Reed
typically restless, and Phlox preoccupied with
getting to his medical lab; Archer was confident
they would be able to deal with the magnitude of
the tragedy. About Hoshi, he was not so sure. He
would have had Phlox talk to her. Phlox had experience in counseling humans, but the doctor would
be consumed with the autopsy. It occurred to
Archer that, as captain, he could have used some

psychological training in order to help his crew; he made a mental note to make a suggestion to Starfleet. A ship's therapist: now, that wasn't such a bad idea.

And, of course, because of his habit of being brutally honest with himself, Archer admitted that, given the fact that *he* had confronted so much death—on the anniversary of his own father's passing—he was not particularly in the mood to eat dinner by himself. Otherwise, he'd have spent the entire time wondering what his father would have done in the same circumstance. Surely Dad would have found a way to save those people. . . .

Come on. He was human. And you're human, too, whether you like it or not. . . .

Archer had invited Trip to make the situation more comfortable, so it wouldn't seem like he, the captain, was worried about Hoshi and Malcolm, but simply interested in discussing the situation. Trip knew nothing about what the landing party had seen on the planet's surface; his presence would allow Hoshi and Malcolm to voice what they'd witnessed, and Archer knew well what a sympathetic listener Trip could be.

"It was pretty hard to take," Archer was telling Trip, who was leaning forward over a scraped-empty bowl of what had been chili with raw chopped onions, to which Trip had enthusiastically applied the greater part of a bottle of hot pepper sauce. With a combined sense of horror and sympathy indigestion, Archer had watched him consume it swiftly, without pause or watery eyes; in fact, Trip hadn't even touched his iced tea until after he'd eaten the entire bowl. Now he sipped it leisurely as he listened intently to his commanding officer's words.

Archer continued, sawing at a piece of uninspiring, synthesized chicken. "Each time T'Pol detected a life sign, by the time we got there, it was too late. . . ." He stopped sawing and sighed, glancing surreptitiously over at Hoshi, hoping she would take the opportunity to open up about how she felt. When she didn't speak, he kept on. "We . . . we made it into a medical facility, where all these people were just sitting together, crowded into a waiting room like cattle. They died like that, just sitting, all of them with calm expressions on their faces, as if they'd just fallen asleep."

"Horrific," Reed sighed, carefully balancing a meatball atop the perfect spaghetti mound he had created. "Like something out of a horror story. Whatever happened to them must have happened too fast for them to fight it. Like an invisible tidal wave, or one of the twenty-first-century designer plagues—so fast, they were alive when they inhaled, and dead by the time they let go the same breath." He paused to poke the meatball with his fork. "Makes you wonder about life. To think we could all be wiped out, our entire civilization, by something so small even our best microscanners can't detect it. . . . The universe is a damnably harsh place."

"I'm sorry, Captain," Hoshi interrupted at last—her first words during the dinner—and pushed the plate from her. "I just don't feel like eating." Archer sensed she was about to stand up and excuse herself, but Trip spoke before she could.

"I don't blame you," he said. "I don't think I could if I'd witnessed the sort of tragedy you just have. It was an awful lot to take in . . . the loss of so many people at once." He shot Reed a warning glance. "Don't listen to the lieutenant here. Things like this don't happen every day."

"An entire world," Archer added softly. He put down his knife.

"I have a theory," Trip said. "The Vulcans are right in one way—"

Archer ogled him owlishly and said, in an attempt at humor, "Call sickbay. The commander's feverish."

Trip *tsk*ed at him, then continued. "No, I'm serious. They're right in the fact that technology overtook us humans awfully quickly. We went from small villages where everybody knew each other to megacities in a matter of a few centuries—before we had the ability to evolve emotionally tougher hides. Think about it: We're emotionally designed to live in small groups, where major tragedies are really uncommon. The death of one person—we're designed to handle that if we're allowed to properly grieve, and have the support of our community. But all of a sudden, our communications advance to where we not only know what's going on in our village, we know what's going on all over the planet—and then the next planet, and the next . . . We're not designed to tolerate all the bad news."

"It makes sense." Archer nodded, hoping to encourage an exchange.

Hoshi frowned down at her glass of water and *ping*ed it by flicking her forefinger off her thumb. "It does. But what happened still happened. Everyone died, and it's just that . . . we were useless down there." She looked up at the men and said, almost argumentatively, "I don't know about you three, sirs, but I came along for this ride because I wanted to make a difference. I wanted to help."

"Sometimes no matter what you do, you *can't* help," Trip said. "At least the people lived well, and had a wonderful culture. From what the captain and Malcolm have said, it sounds like they all died peacefully."

Hoshi shook her head. "Not one man."

"Uggh." Reed shuddered. "That's true. He had a ghastly time of it."

Archer turned to Trip. "In one of the medical treatment rooms, we found a female survivor—at least, she was alive when we found her. There was a male who'd been standing over her bed—her doctor, maybe—and he'd died and fallen on top of her. When we lifted him up, we saw his face. . . ."

"It was awful, Commander," Hoshi said, at last showing some of the anguish she'd been trying to hold in. "His expression was contorted, as if he'd been angry, so angry at something, and so tormented by it. . . ."

The remembered image filled Archer with sadness; at the same time, he felt a sudden inspiration as to how to encourage Hoshi. "It was a horrible thing to have to see. That's why I'm glad we have you, Hoshi. All their logs, including those we found in that hospital room—you'll be able to help solve the mystery."

"But it's too late to help them, sir," Hoshi countered miserably. "That was my point. . . ."

"Maybe," Archer interjected. "But the records they left will help others, might stop the same thing from happening again. You'll be helping them leave a legacy."

At that, Hoshi lifted her chin and gave him an appreciative look. "Thank you, Captain. You know, you really shouldn't worry about me. I'll be all right once I get to work. Besides, it had to have been just as hard on you to see what we did."

Archer felt a hint of a wry smile make its way to his lips.

Reed leaned forward, watching the captain expectantly, apparently hoping for similar encouragement; Archer's smile became fixed as he gave Reed a little shrug. The smile vanished quickly as the door opened.

T'Pol's slender form appeared in the hatchway.

"Come in," Archer said warmly, grateful for the rescue.

But the Vulcan lingered tentatively in the entry. "I had hoped to speak with you alone, sir. Now is clearly not an appropriate time. May I make an appointment?"

"No need." Archer rose and nodded at his dinner companions. "If you'll excuse me . . ."

"I did not mean to interrupt you," T'Pol insisted, but Archer was already beside her, and led her out into the empty common dining room. Once there, he faced her squarely.

"What can I do for you, Sub-Commander?"

"Sir," she said smoothly, and though her finely drawn features remained composed in her customary placid expression, Archer sensed her unease. "I have come to a decision regarding my role in the death of the last survivor on the planet's surface."

Once again, the captain considered the death of the alien from the Vulcan's point of view: despite T'Pol's apparent lack of reaction, the incident had had a profound effect on her; and while he felt some degree of success in terms of helping Hoshi to deal emotionally with her trauma, he had no

idea how to counsel a Vulcan—if, indeed, counseling would do any good. But he knew that T'Pol
had to be reminded of the time, long ago, when
she'd been forced to kill a Vulcan smuggler in
self-defense. It had been very difficult for her to
come to grips with it then. . . . He hoped, in this
case, it was easier for her now.

"T'Pol," he said earnestly, "as Hoshi said, it
wasn't your fault that the alien died. I was ready
to fire at him myself; you just beat me to the
punch. There was no way of predicting that he
was going to—"

She interrupted him. "I directly caused his
death, Captain."

"Even so, you couldn't have known it would
happen. And the alternative was to let him kill
Hoshi. Like I said, I was about to fire at him myself."

"But you are a human. I am a Vulcan."

Archer fought not to rankle at the implication.
"So I've noticed."

"As a Vulcan, I am responsible for living my life
in as nonviolent a way as possible. I had several
alternatives for rescuing Hoshi instead of firing
my weapon; had I relied on my intelligence rather
than my instincts, I would have realized the possible danger of stunning the alien."

"What alternatives?" Archer was honestly perplexed. "It all happened so fast. . . ."

She did not answer his question, but instead

continued, "I have reflected deeply on the situation. The only way to properly maintain my Vulcan ethics is to return to the strictest original teachings of Surak. For that reason, I cannot condone violence of any kind; and for that reason, I must inform you that I will no longer carry or use any type of weapon."

"Sub-Commander . . ." Archer did his best to be understanding. "What happened was an accident. You couldn't have prevente d it."

"I could have, and should have. I have grown lax in my discipline."

He bowed his head, considering his next words carefully, trying to curtail the mounting frustration he suddenly felt. He realized that she had not blamed her "laxness" on being surrounded by humans—but he felt the implication, however subtle, was there.

Yet Archer also knew he had a chip on his shoulder, especially on this day, of all days: Henry Archer had died without being able to see *Enterprise* leave spacedock because the Vulcans had delayed the launch, stating that humans weren't "emotionally ready" for contact with other lifeforms. *You've put that all behind you,* Archer reminded himself. T'Pol had made it clear enough that she was now voluntarily aboard *Enterprise;* she had proven her respect for her fellow officers enough times.

"T'Pol . . . you've become a real part of this

crew. And down there on the planet's surface, you may well have saved Hoshi's life. What if I need you to protect this vessel? What if, say, I'm down on the planet's surface and you're in charge of this ship, and *Enterprise* is suddenly attacked? Are you saying you won't retaliate defensively? That you won't protect yourself or my crew?"

"Correct," she replied evenly.

Archer's lips parted in amazement; unable to believe what he had just heard, he pressed. Certainly she would not endanger *Enterprise!* "You would disobey a direct order from me to use force?"

T'Pol's tone was respectful but firm. "I would, sir."

"That's . . . That's . . ." Archer's anger caused the word to stick in his throat. He struggled and at last managed to gather himself, but he no longer bothered to maintain a sympathetic expression. "That's all, Sub-Commander. We'll discuss this further, after we've both had a chance to think about things."

She opened her mouth to speak; he already knew what she was going to say. *I have already thought about things, Captain. I have already made my decision.* Before she could utter a word, he turned on his heel and went back into the captain's dining room.

Hoshi and Trip were in relaxed midconversation, with Reed listening avidly, when Archer retook his seat—but at the sight of him, they both fell silent; Hoshi's dark eyes grew wide. He was fuming, Archer realized, and doing a poor job of hiding it; in fact, Hoshi stood up at once and said, "I appreciate the chance to talk about what happened down on the planet's surface, sir. If you'll excuse me, I'll be heading for my quarters. . . ."

Reed cleared his throat. "Yes. Yes, I'll be going as well, sir. With your permission."

Archer gave a sullen nod.

"Bye," Hoshi told Trip, shot an uncertain glance at the captain, then eagerly made her way for the door; Reed followed suit.

Once they were gone, Trip gave the captain a good look up and down at finally said, "Whoa. So just exactly what did she say that got you riled?"

Archer did not need to ask which "she" Tucker referred to. "Dammit, Trip, she just told me to my face that she'd refuse my direct order."

"Hold on, now . . . Back it up, Cap'n. T'Pol didn't just come up to you and say . . ."

Archer let go an exasperated puff of air. "She stunned an alien who attacked Hoshi, and he wound up dying seconds after she shot him."

"T'Pol shot first?"

Archer nodded.

"Ouch. That must have gotten Reed's goat. Outgunned by a Vulcan."

"A Vulcan who blames herself for the alien's death," Archer persisted, ignoring Trip's amusement.

"But she couldn't have known he'd die," Trip said. "If her phase pistol was set on stun . . ."

"It was. But it's worse than that. He was the last survivor. The only one left of his race . . . maybe our last chance to solve the mystery of what killed them."

"Well, now, that I can understand." Trip's tone was mollifying. "And . . . ?"

"And so she feels she's broken the Vulcan moral code against killing . . . I guess we humans are a bad influence, so she feels the need to purify herself by returning to a stricter version of Surak's code. No violence even in the name of self-defense. I asked her point-blank whether she would use defensive weaponry if the ship was under attack, and she said no." Archer turned to his friend. "I mean, come on, Trip. I asked her if she'd defend a crewmate or the ship if given a direct order to do so, and she said no. And that's just plain insubordination."

"So it is," Trip admitted, nodding noncommittally. For a time, he said nothing, and then he asked, "You ever kill anyone, Cap'n?"

Archer didn't answer; he stared at his friend, taken aback by the question. He did not mention T'Pol's experience with killing Jossen, as she had revealed the fact to him in strictest confidence.

"Didn't think so," Trip said. "Think how she must feel about it, raised in a culture that values nonviolence above all else—and now she's gone and reacted instinctively, and killed someone.

Even if you and I knew the guy was dead anyway. And think about it—the last survivor of a race . . . not an easy thing to deal with."

"But even the Vulcans allow killing in self-defense. It'd be absurd not to. You've got the right to protect yourself from someone who wishes violence on you, don't you? Even Surak—"

"Hold on right there," Tucker said. "Surak's earliest teachings taught complete nonviolence. Very Gandhi-esque, very turn-the-other-cheek. If they strike you down, rely on your survivors to take your place and speak out for peace. But never raise your hand against another."

"Really?" Archer's interest was piqued.

"The Vulcans'll never admit it, but they squabble about the correct interpretation of Surak's teachings on this matter all the time."

"So where do you get all your secret information on the Vulcans from?" Archer teased.

"I'll never tell," Trip said. "Got to keep my sources hidden." He paused; when he spoke again, his tone was once again serious. "Look, give T'Pol some leeway on this. She probably feels a whole lot of good old-fashioned guilt over this, even though she'll never admit it. She's bound to come around."

"I'll give her time," Archer said. "So long as she does nothing to jeopardize my people or my ship." He almost said *my father's ship*, and caught himself only at the last moment.

51

Three

"O-*AH*-NEE," Hoshi repeated, staring mesmerized into her viewer in the small laboratory set up next to sickbay. Frozen there was the image of an alien who had spoken the warning that *Enterprise* had encountered before the landing party had gone down to the planet's surface. Odd, after seeing so many of his peers dead, to see a healthy male alien alert, his face animated by the concern reflected in his resonant voice.

"O-*ah*-nee," Hoshi repeated again, mimicking the speaker. After two hours' intense work, she had determined, after repeated viewings of several tapes, that this particular message was intended for any off-worlders who happened upon the stricken planet. And the Oani (such was her phonetic spelling of the word) were the name of the people; their world was Oan.

But she was having some difficulty replicating the precise pronunciation herself of the interesting pronunciation of the *ah* syllable; it combined a glottal stop with a click, causing her to use the muscles deep in her throat. Less than a minute before, she had practiced so vigorously that one of the medical aides in the next lab had come by for fear she was retching. She'd done her best to try to explain what she was doing, but the aide left with a disbelieving air.

Ah, the joys of being a linguist. True, she merely needed to transcribe the phoneme into the computer, but there was deep personal satisfaction for her when she finally got the sound exactly right herself.

"O-*ah*-nee."

That accomplished, Hoshi entered her rough translation into the computer, then recorded it onto tape so that she could play it back for the others.

"We are the Oani. A warning to visitors: we suffer from an unknown disease. Please protect yourselves. If you can offer assistance, contact us and we will transmit medical data."

Again, it was rough; Hoshi knew nothing about the culture save what she had seen on the planet's surface, so she had no idea whether the warning held any subtext or unspoken assumptions. Her feeling—a perfectly nonscientific hunch—was that the warning was as straightforward as it appeared, and that the Oani were indeed concerned enough about outsiders to warn them to stay clear of the planet.

But had they ever discovered what had killed them?

Hoshi removed the disk of the warning and put in the first tape they'd discovered in the medical facility, in the room where Dr. Phlox had struggled unsuccessfully to keep the woman alive. Hoshi knew it was her job to study the tape—but she felt an enormous reluctance to face the image of the man who had died with an expression of such hatred, such fury on his features.

But the instant his living image appeared on her viewer, Hoshi was mesmerized, all discomfort forgotten. Here was the living man, his expression alert, keen with concern, his lashless dark eyes round and so luminous that Hoshi found them attractive, even by human standards. The first entry he made was terse, too brief for her to make much of; she replayed it again and again until it began to make sense in context of all she'd heard before.

Uroqa: that was his name, and he gave what was probably a date and time. Hoshi fast-forwarded and confirmed the repetition of the name and the date/time, which varied just enough. These were precisely what Dr. Phlox and Captain Archer had

54

hoped, medical log entries, and she sat entranced, listening to Uroqa's deep bass—deeper tones than a human was capable of producing. Given the urgency of his tone, these logs probably commenced at some point after the medical crisis had already begun.

This time, Hoshi played the first entry at normal speed, listening carefully. She began to pick out certain words—*medical, disease*—enough times to convince her she had the proper translation. It always amazed her, no matter how many times she began to interpret a new language, how effortlessly and swiftly her brain put the pieces of the linguistic puzzle together; as a child, she had taken her ability for granted, and assumed that everyone could read backward and upside down, and made up their own secret alphabets for sending coded messages to friends in school. Early on, Starfleet Intelligence had made efforts to recruit her, but she had no interest in politics or espionage. Languages were for learning about new cultures, for making new friends.

She watched as Uroqa made his swift, tense report—and then he glanced up as another person entered the room.

Hoshi let out a small gasp of recognition: it was the female who had been alive when the landing party had found her—alive, beneath Uroqa's body. She said his name—with alien intonation, to be sure, but Hoshi heard the tenderness in her voice, saw the sudden brightness in Uroqa's eyes when he glanced up and saw her there.

"*Kano,*" he said, and spoke to her softly, his tone now one of gentle reproach. Hoshi did not know the meaning of each word, but she understood him all too well: *You should not be here, in the midst of all this danger.*

Hoshi's throat tightened suddenly; she realized she was in danger of weeping and blinked rapidly, determined to remain the scientist. Now was not the time to be moved.

She had permitted Captain Archer to talk her into signing aboard *Enterprise* very quickly; it had all been very exciting, the promise of travel and the chance to meet aliens from other cultures, and learn their languages. But it had never occurred to her that they would encounter such a horrific situation—that her skills would be put to such grim use, and the minor joy of learning a new tongue was profoundly eclipsed by the sorrowful circumstance. It had been very difficult to maintain concentration. Now she was struggling not to cry.

At that precise instant, Captain Archer appeared in the hatchway, a hint of a smile on his lips, despite the fact the he looked tired. "Hoshi. Anything so far?"

"Captain," she said, composing herself at once. She rose from her chair. "Not a lot, sir, but I can give you a better translation of the warning."

She played her tape back for him, and he listened to it thoughtfully. "Good work. Anything else?"

She nodded. "We're in luck. Those tapes we found in the medical facility—you were right. They're medical logs. I'm just getting started with those, but the beginning's always the hardest part. Once I gain more facility with their language, the work will go a lot faster. Right now the logs indicate they didn't know what was happening to them."

It was Archer's turn to nod, rather glumly.

"Sir," Hoshi asked, "has Doctor Phlox discovered anything new?"

"No word so far," Archer said. "He's my next stop. I'll let you know if there's anything."

"Thanks." Hoshi smiled.

On his way out, Archer paused to glance at the image of the two aliens on her viewer; a look of recognition passed over his features, followed by a darker emotion that he quickly stifled. Hoshi glanced at him curiously. Months of serving together at close quarters left her sensitive to the other officers' moods, and there had been a gray cloud hovering over the captain even before they had gone down to the doomed planet Oan.

"I wish I could tell you more, Captain," Phlox said, before Archer had fully set foot inside sickbay. The doctor stood over a diagnostic bed where the corpse of the last female to die reposed, covered by a layer of nonpermeable film. His back was to Archer; apparently he had recognized the captain's footfall or done a good job of guessing. "I've spent the entire night studying their morphology and physiology, and other than that slight difference in electrolytes I detected when we were on the planet's surface, I've found nothing to account for their deaths. No microbes, no parasites, no sign of poisoning or radiation, no exposure to weaponry that we're familiar with . . ." He turned to face the captain; either the lack of sleep or the frustration had made its mark on him. His normally pink features were sallow; shadows had appeared in the folds beneath his eyes. "To be quite honest, Captain, I really don't know what further tests to perform. Short of going down to the planet's surface, I—"

"They called themselves the Oani," Archer interrupted. It was a non sequitur, but he could think of nothing to say in response to Phlox's discouraging report. It wasn't that he was worried about his crew contracting the mysterious illness—he wasn't—but he felt he owed a solution to the Oanis. It would be simply too sad, too meaningless for an entire race to die off without that legacy he had spoken to Hoshi of.

"Oani," Phlox repeated thoughtfully, and gazed down at the sealed corpse. "I'm sorry I didn't get to meet them under better circumstances."

Archer opened his mouth to agree, but at the last moment changed his mind and asked, "What about the male who attacked Hoshi? And the one with the contorted features? Was there insanity or rage associated with whatever killed them?"

Phlox sighed. "I wish I could speak with certainty, Captain, but at the moment, I find myself with more questions than answers. However, my best guess is that no, the apparently violent impulse that overtook the poor man had more to do with a coincidental dementia brought on by organic brain disease. As for the gentleman with the disturbing expression, he showed no signs of insanity; he was quite healthy in all respects until his death."

As the doctor finished his sentence, T'Pol's voice filtered through the companel.

"T'Pol to sickbay."

The doctor moved to the bulkhead and tapped the control. "Phlox here."

"Doctor, have you heard anything unusual?"

"I beg your pardon?"

"Anything unusual," T'Pol repeated blandly. "I take it by your reply you have not. I'm looking for Captain Archer. Have you seen him?"

Phlox turned and made a sweeping gesture at Archer, who stepped to the companel.

"Archer here."

"Captain . . ." Perhaps it was Archer's imagination, but he detected a curious undercurrent of anticipation in the Vulcan's tone. "Would you please report to the bridge? And could Ensign Sato accompany you?"

The captain frowned, immediately concerned, but intrigued by the request to bring Hoshi. "Is anything wrong?"

"Negative, sir. We seem to be receiving a unique form of alien contact."

"We'll be there," Archer said before T'Pol had completely uttered her last word, then punched the control and turned on his heel in one swift move, leaving Phlox to gaze after him.

As Archer and Hoshi stepped onto the bridge, T'Pol immediately vacated the command chair—but did not return to her post. Both Reed at tactical and Mayweather at the helm were watching the encounter with great interest—and more than a little anxiety, Archer judged.

"Captain," she acknowledged, then turned her attention to Hoshi. "Ensign Sato . . . do you hear anything unusual?"

Hoshi paused to concentrate; her gaze grew distant, then she frowned slightly and said, "Maybe. Do you think one of the subwarp engines is straining a bit?"

T'Pol's lips compressed themselves a bit more firmly; this was apparently not the reply she had hoped to hear. And Archer was no longer in the mood for any more mysteries.

"Out with it, Sub-Commander. Exactly what do you hear?"

"Vulcan," she answered.

The captain did a slight double take.

"More specifically," T'Pol added, "a female voice speaking Vulcan. It identifies itself as an amorphous entity, composed entirely of energy particles, yet possessing consciousness. It asks—"

As she was talking, Archer flashed on the image of the mad Oani male attacking Hoshi and felt a sudden chill descend over him. He and the exolinguist shared an uncomfortable glance. Was T'Pol now going insane? Had the unidentified plague found its way aboard *Enterprise*?

Relax, Archer chided himself. *From what we know, all but two of those people died calmly.*

Nevertheless, he interrupted T'Pol. "Sub-Commander, you may very well be hearing the voice of an invisible alien entity that for some reason, the rest of us can't detect. But I think it's reasonable"—he emphasized the word—"to ask that you report to sickbay and have yourself checked out."

T'Pol lifted her eyebrows in mild protest. "I assure you, Captain, I feel quite well. Should you wish to verify the truth of what I am saying, we need merely scan for the existence of the creature in the area of space it claims to be located."

"Then do it," Archer said.

T'Pol's full lips parted; after a slight hesitation, she said, "According to the coordinates, the entity is currently beyond the range of our scanners. We need to leave Kappa Xi Two's orbit."

A gruesome image flashed in Archer's mind: *Enterprise* as a ghost ship, aimlessly asail through space with her bridge crew sitting dead at their posts. Who knew what other life-forms they might expose to the mysterious plague? And if the Vulcans came looking for them . . . He stopped the thought at once and stated firmly, "I won't risk leaving orbit until I can be sure we won't spread the disease further. Report to sickbay, Sub-Commander. That's an order."

He saw the flicker of resistance in her eyes; but she at last nodded calmly and said, "Very well, Captain."

He, Reed, and Hoshi watched her leave.

"Return to your work," Archer told the exolinguist. "We might need your help sooner than you think."

"So it begins," Mayweather muttered—not quite softly enough. Archer heard and turned to him in irritation.

"Ensign?"

Mayweather stiffened at his post. "Yes, sir?"

"Do me a favor and knock off the dramatics. We've got enough excitement as it is."

"Yes, sir."

* * *

An anxious hour later, Archer sat in his command chair and listened to Phlox via companel.

"She checks out perfectly healthy, Captain," the doctor said. "And as far as I can tell, she's completely rational. I detect no psychosis. I'd say her claim about an energy-based entity merits examination. I'm sending her back up to the bridge."

"Thank God," Archer breathed. He could sense the others on the bridge relaxing around him: Mayweather's shoulders dropped significantly; Reed emitted an audible sigh. "So she shows no sign of the disease."

"Correct." The Denobulan paused. "Of course, that doesn't mean that she hasn't been affected by whatever killed the Oanis."

"Wait a minute, Doctor. You just said she was perfectly healthy."

"That's what all her readings indicate," the doctor countered. "But remember, the people down on the planet's surface showed no sign of disease, either."

"So any of us could be infected." Archer watched as Mayweather's shoulders tensed upward a quarter-inch.

"I'm afraid it's possible. Although at this time, there's no indication that's happened."

Archer sighed. "In other words, we simply won't know until the first of us gets sick. You know, I really prefer it when things are a little more black-and-white."

"Black-and-white . . . ? Ah, a colorful—or should I say, monochromatic—metaphor. Well, I'm sorry I can only give you gray at the moment, Captain."

"Please, don't apologize." Archer shook his head, even though Phlox couldn't see him. "You've worked harder than any of us at trying to solve this; we're all in your debt."

"I appreciate that, sir."

As Phlox's words filtered through the com-panel, T'Pol stepped through the lift doors onto the bridge.

"Keep up the good work, Doctor," Archer said. "Archer out." T'Pol had moved to her station; the captain turned to her. "So, are you still hearing the voice of this . . . entity?"

She faced him, her posture formal, a bit stiff. "I am, sir. However, Doctor Phlox has verified that I am not hallucinating . . ."

"I'm not questioning that, T'Pol. I'd like to know whether you're able to communicate with it. To explain why we can't leave planetary orbit to go meet it."

She tilted her head, revealing a high, angular cheekbone. "I shall try, Captain." She closed her eyes and concentrated, a slight crease forming be-tween her upswept brows. After a minute, she opened her eyes again. "It has already received the message; it is monitoring our vessel and knows what you have said."

Archer was not at all sure he liked the sound of

that, but remained quiet as T'Pol continued: "It says that it already passed by the planet, and has been exposed to their disease—but is immune because it is not, like us, a carbon-based life-form. However, it does have considerable medical knowledge based on its studies, and wishes to offer its help in discovering the cause of the Oani's deaths."

"Fair enough," Archer said. "We can use whatever help we can get. Can it communicate directly with Doctor Phlox?"

T'Pol closed her eyes again; this time she frowned, then opened them and looked over at the captain almost immediately. "Negative. It claims to be able to communicate only with me."

"It makes no sense," Archer says. "If it's 'conversing' directly with you in Vulcan—and you're silently 'thinking' messages to it—then it has to be telepathic. So why couldn't it communicate with Phlox in Denobulan?"

"Maybe it's transmitting at a frequency only T'Pol can hear," Travis Mayweather offered from the helm. "Vulcan's the lingua franca of a number of spacefaring races."

Archer considered this, but remained skeptical; however, any offer of help by any being who had already been exposed to the illness that killed the Oanis could not be ignored. He opened his mouth to tell T'Pol this when the Vulcan spoke first.

"It also states that it is, like us, a spacefaring

entity on a mission of exploration. It wishes to know whether we are interested in exchanging information about our cultures." T'Pol's expression was as animated as Archer had ever seen it, her eyes especially bright; clearly, her scientific curiosity had been piqued. In his mind, he heard Trip Tucker's voice saying, *A Vulcan in love* . . . "It is asking permission to approach us in order to facilitate such an exchange."

The captain wasted no more time in arguing against the opportunity. "Tell it to come."

T'Pol nodded; this time, she merely unfocused her gaze for an instant, then bent over her viewer. After a time, she straightened and said, "Unusual energy configuration approaching. Currently located twenty-five hundred kilome-ters from the ship at coordinates seven-oh-five-zero."

It had moved with warp speed. Just to make sure, Archer stood behind her and tried to peer into her viewer; she sensed him and, without taking offense, stepped aside so that he could get a better look.

"Sir," Malcolm Reed interjected, his voice filled with tension. "Are you sure you don't want to activate the hull plating?"

T'Pol turned toward him. "It would do no good, Lieutenant. At any rate, the creature is benign."

"*Claims* to be benign," Reed corrected her. "And you can't be sure that activating the plating would do no good."

"Not yet, Lieutenant," Archer said. "If this thing meant us harm, why would it be asking our permission for anything?" He paused, then bent forward over T'Pol's viewer, his vague and private relief that his science officer truly wasn't mad mixing with a sudden intense curiosity. "Will you look at *that?*" No image appeared on the viewer, only a digital readout of various forms of harmless radiation, mixed with electromagnetic pulses, which had gathered into a dense cloudlike formation.

"Sentient," T'Pol said, studying it alongside him, clearly fascinated. "Yet totally amorphous."

"On screen," Archer told Mayweather, who obliged immediately.

The sight of it caused Archer to rise from his chair. Whatever he had expected to see, this was not it: a roiling play of energy that looked like dappled light on breaking turquoise waves of water; for an instant, he thought of the island planet and its seas below.

Conscious energy. *Why does it surprise me so to find it in the universe?* Archer wondered. *The physicists have always said we're just light in frozen form . . .*

To the screen, he said aloud, "Greetings from the crew of the starship *Enterprise*. We appreciate your offer of help in discovering what killed the inhabitants of" —he paused, struggling to re-

member what Hoshi had called the planet—
"Oan."

"The entity returns your greetings, Captain,"
T'Pol answered immediately behind him. Her
gaze, too, was fixed on the screen. "It asks permission to come aboard to work directly with
Doctor Phlox. I will serve as translator."

"Why does it need to come aboard?" Archer
asked. "It seems to communicate just fine from
this distance."

"It can 'hear' us, but it cannot see our diagnostic equipment or know the results of any tests
Doctor Phlox has run. Nor can it examine the tissue samples."

"But it's huge," Archer said, still staring at the
viewscreen. "Look at it. How many hundreds of
kilometers across is it?"

T'Pol paused, then replied, "It says that it can
condense itself to humanoid size in order to facilitate working with us. It is not easy for it to accomplish this—it will take it some time in order
to do so. But once in condensed form, it can remain thus indefinitely."

The captain hesitated. He had no reason to
deny letting this creature aboard his vessel, especially if it had already been exposed to the illness
and was immune, as it claimed. Yet breaking
quarantine left him enormously uncomfortable.

At the same time, he realized that they were
being offered an incredible opportunity, not just

in terms of communicating with a radically different species with a great deal of spacefaring knowledge, but also in terms of learning more about the Oani's medical disaster.

And that's what *Enterprise* was here for.

"Very well," he said finally. "Tell it to come aboard."

Four

ARCHER HAD SCARCELY uttered the words when the shimmering vision on the viewscreen disappeared, leaving in its place the blue-green island world, Oan, against the backdrop of space, and the glow from the more distant sun the humans had labeled Kappa Xi.

Yet by the time the captain blinked and opened his eyes once more, the roiling blue-green energy field appeared once more—this time, in a condensed, more vibrantly colored column, roughly the size and width of a human male, just in front of Travis Mayweather's helm console.

Mayweather, born in space and as blasé about new experiences as anyone Archer had ever met, craned his neck forward to gawk openly at the creature, and when he glanced over his shoulder to gauge the reaction of the others, his dark skin bathed in the alien's glow, his eyes were as round as Archer's.

"You ever heard of anything like this?" Archer asked him softly.

"No, sir," Mayweather breathed, then turned back to stare at the creature.

As for Reed, he took a step forward from his station, his eyes also widened by curiosity, but in his expression was distrust; instinctively, his right hand moved for the phase pistol he no longer wore.

The captain gathered himself and stepped toward the semitransparent, pulsating sea of energy. He wanted nothing more than to ask, *How did you do that?*, but the considerations of diplomacy came before any improvements to the transporter. "Welcome aboard. I'm Captain Jonathan Archer of the starship *Enterprise*." Extending a hand was out of the question; the creature was the general size of a human, but other than that, was entirely without form. There was definitely nothing there to grab hold of.

T'Pol moved forward from her station to stand beside the captain. "It has no name for itself, but it thinks of itself as a wanderer, and asks that we address it as such."

"Very well . . . Wanderer. I'd like to escort you down to sickbay so that you can confer with Doctor Phlox, our chief medical officer. Will you accompany me?"

T'Pol made the slightest sound, which Archer interpreted as an extremely courteous clearing of her throat. "Captain . . . Wanderer requests that I be present at all times to serve as translator."

"Oh . . . yes. Of course."

"And," the Vulcan added, "it says it is 'anxious' to meet with Doctor Phlox, as it has important information to share with him."

Archer brightened at once; while the creature wore no expression, it suddenly appeared to him as wise and beneficent. Its blue-green glow seemed as warm and radiant as a smile. "Then let's get moving."

"Wonderful," Doctor Phlox said, his face bathed in Wanderer's azure glow as he stood in front of the sealed, decontaminated corpse of an Oani. The Denobulan's eyes were bright with excitement, his tone even more animated than normal at the sight of such an unusual being. To T'Pol, he said, "Ask it—may I touch it? Study it?"

"Wanderer has already agreed to a cultural exchange," the Vulcan replied.

"Doctor," Archer interjected, "there's a more serious issue to deal with first. Wanderer says it can help you find out what killed the Oanis." The captain himself had hundreds of questions for the alien: Where had it come from? Were there others like it? It referred to itself using a neuter pronoun—how did it reproduce? Yet, staring at the bronze-colored body on the bed behind Phlox, Archer felt an anxious sense of urgency.

"Indeed," T'Pol agreed, most seriously. And then, with that wry, infinitesimal quirk at one corner of her mouth that betrayed a startling sense of humor, she added, "Besides, Wanderer warns against your touching it. It believes that its energy patterns might cause you to feel something akin to an electrical shock."

Phlox did not actually release a disappointed sigh, but Archer got the clear impression that he repressed one. "Very well," the Denobulan said. "Let us get started, then."

Archer lingered for only a moment—long enough to watch as Phlox gestured the swirling energy column behind him, toward the dead Oani, long enough to stare with amazement as the creature compacted itself even further, and began, slowly, to seep *inside* the Oani's body, lighting it up from within with an iridescent bluish glow.

He forced himself to leave. All he could do now was return to the bridge, and wait, and hope.

Meanwhile, Hoshi crouched over the hooded viewer in one of the labs near sickbay. She'd been staring at the images for some time, and finally straightened to rub the spot between her eyebrows, to fight the eyestrain headache that was just beginning.

The incident with T'Pol still worried her; she'd

been too busy to check on the Vulcan's status—
and each time she thought of calling to sickbay to
see how T'Pol was doing, she instead redoubled
her efforts at translating. If T'Pol was sick, then
Hoshi needed to work faster; and even if T'Pol
wasn't sick, she, Hoshi, needed to work fast anyway, because who knew when the illness might
strike one of them?

The thought made her stop rubbing her forehead and lean over the viewer again, feeling its
glow illumine her face.

At least she had made enough progress so that
she no longer needed to stop each few words and
translate. Now she was listening to Uroqa's medical
logs, compelled by the image of the bronze-skinned
Oani, his dark eyes naturally liquid and shining,
more so than human eyes ever could. He was thick-
necked, broad-shouldered, muscular, brimming
with strength and life; but his voice, a resonant
baritone, was tentative, filled with concern.

"It is not in the air, not in the earth, not in the
sea," he said. "Therefore, it must be in us. Is it a
microbe, too small to be detected by our present
filters?" he asked thoughtfully, with such a natural, conversational air that Hoshi felt he was
speaking directly to her. "And if it *is* a microbe,
who am I to say I have the right to end its life ar-
tificially? Who am I to claim the life of another
piece of creation, no matter how small? Who am I
to interfere with the natural order of things?"

"But your people are dying," Hoshi said in English to the small screen. "Do you have the right to let such a lower life-form kill them?"

"Reverence for life dictates that we must not kill," Uroqa continued, almost as if in reply. "Yet how can I let my people die? All beings must compromise to live in peace—but how do we compromise with a being whose existence depends on our death? When does our right to live supersede another's?"

Uroqa rose and stepped across the room to a place Hoshi instantly recognized: the shimmering sea green nutrient bed where the dying Oani woman rested—the one Dr. Phlox hadn't been able to revive.

"I must save her," Uroqa said simply, and gently took her limp hand in his own.

Hoshi snapped off the viewer, fighting off emotion. Periodically, she had translated and condensed the medical logs into purely pertinent data for Phlox's computer, omitting the unnecessary personal information—including the sad story of Uroqa and his stricken mate, Kano. Now seemed like a good time to take a physical as well as mental break and walk her latest findings over to sickbay.

She sighed, popped her disk out of the computer, and headed down the corridor. As a scientist, she told herself, she needed to develop a tougher hide: watching Uroqa's logs with full knowledge of his fate was taking too much of an emotional toll on her, and she needed to remain detached if she was to be of use. It didn't help matters that Uroqa was so personable, or that his relationship with his mate was so tender: Hoshi was beginning to look on him as a friend, and that, she knew, was dangerous.

He had a good life, an ethical life, she reminded herself. *He knew real love, and he was devoted to peace.*

But she couldn't help being sad. The universe was diminished by the loss of a race of such compassionate beings; it would have been wonderful to have met them when they were still alive.

Yet what, she asked herself silently, *could have filled a peaceful person like Uroqa with such fury in his final moments?*

By that time, Hoshi found herself in sickbay with no memory of having made the walk there; and what she saw, when she walked through Phlox's office back into the treatment area, made her stop in her tracks.

As T'Pol and the doctor stood at either side of the diagnostic bed, watching, *something* moved through Kona's corpse, as if it had burrowed inside. Hoshi stared, aghast, as Kano's spine began to undulate, and a strange blue-green glow radiated from within her, through the pale gauze of her long, loose tunic at the waist. The blue-green pulse moved upward, through her neck, causing her throat to constrict, her lipless mouth to open and emit the same strange light. At last, her entire, once-passive face began to glow as well, and to Hoshi's horror, her dark eyes popped open, agleam with shimmering turquoise.

"No!" Hoshi cried, in spite of herself, then firmly bit her lip. Whatever was happening here was sacrilege; Uroqa would have been outraged. Yet Phlox watched the procedure with hopeful fascination, and T'Pol with serene detachment.

T'Pol turned to see her at once, and immediately went to her side.

"What is it?" Hoshi asked, lowering her voice. Her outburst left her somewhat embarrassed; obviously the doctor and T'Pol would only do something that would help discover what had killed the Oani. Yet, after seeing how Uroqa had cared for Kano, Hoshi could not help feeling protective about her, even if a body was all that was left.

T'Pol's cool demeanor never flickered. "This is Wanderer," she said, gesturing toward the body. "The energy field that contacted me. Apparently, it has abilities that can discover the cause of the Oani's extinction. It has merged with the corpse in a diagnostic procedure. I am here in order to translate for the entity."

"Oh. Good. Well, I'm glad that you're all right," Hoshi said awkwardly. She had no desire to move any closer to the strange creature inside Kano's body, so she handed the Vulcan the disk. "Here. Would you give this to Doctor Phlox? It's the latest compilation I made of the Oani medical logs."

T'Pol tilted her head somewhat quizzically, as though she were going to question why Hoshi didn't give it to the doctor herself—but the human woman didn't give her the chance to ask. She turned swiftly and headed out of sickbay without another look back.

Perhaps she should have been fascinated: after all, here was an amazing creature, unlike anything the humans had ever seen—but Hoshi wanted nothing to do with it. There was something irreverent, even callous about the way it had moved inside Kano's body . . . something that left Hoshi filled with a curious foreboding that she could not explain.

On the bridge, Archer finally got the call he'd been waiting for.

"Captain . . . Phlox here in sickbay."

"Report, Doctor." Archer was literally sitting on the edge of his seat; it had been a perfectly quiet shift, and there'd been nothing to distract himself with, other than his own thoughts and the sight of the blue-green world on the viewscreen.

"Wanderer has explained to me what killed the Oanis."

"Wonderful!"

Phlox sounded doubtful. "I wouldn't necessarily describe it in those terms, Captain."

"Explain."

"Apparently, solar winds caused a shift in their stratosphere, which permitted a rare form of harmful radiation which had always been present to kill them."

"What type of radiation?"

"Wanderer isn't being specific in this regard, Captain. It has no name for the radiation, though it's extremely good at sensing different types. It has no name because *we* have no name for it—we haven't discovered it yet, nor have the Vulcans, so it doesn't know how to explain it to T'Pol. As Wanderer said, it's extremely rare. And . . ." Phlox paused ominously.

"Say it, Doctor," Archer demanded, even though he knew he did not want to hear the answer.

"And it's fatal to humans, Vulcans, Denobulans . . . most humanoids, in fact, if exposure is sustained."

Archer let go a silent breath, as though he'd been firmly struck below the breastbone. He had insisted on keeping the ship in orbit around Oan, for fear of spreading a disease. "How much exposure?"

Phlox did not answer for a beat, and Archer demanded with anger—anger directed entirely at himself—"*How much* exposure, Doctor?"

"I just had T'Pol ask Wanderer. Apparently,

Wanderer doesn't know. This is its first encounter with humans."

"Well, ask Wanderer what it can do to help us avoid this type of radiation sickness."

Another pause, then Phlox responded, "Wanderer says it can do nothing. If any of us are going to be ill, we'll probably start showing signs soon."

"Nothing? Come on, Doctor. This entity is some sort of radiation specialist—and even us humans have learned how to deal with other types of radiation sickness. Surely it has some advice on this rare type."

"I'm afraid not, Captain. It says that it understands radiation perfectly well, but doesn't understand why humanoid bodies react as they do to it. It's coming from an entirely different perspective. . . ."

"Well, it's going to have to learn some new perspectives," Archer said, "if it wants that 'cultural exchange.' Archer out." He punched the control on his companel, then stared forward at the viewscreen, where the blue-green island world rotated lazily on its axis. "Ensign Mayweather. Plot a course out of here."

The ensign's young features reflected the concern on the captain's own. "Direction, sir?"

"Surprise me," Archer said flatly, then pounded the underside of his fist on the companel again. "Commander Tucker."

"Yes, sir." Trip's voice filtered up from engineering. Normally, he would have responded far more casually, or put a humorous emphasis on the *sir*, but he clearly sensed from Archer's tone that this was all business.

"I need warp four, Trip. We've got to get out of here as fast as possible."

Trip didn't even pause. "You've got it coming, Captain. I'll signal you back when she's ready."

Archer flipped a different toggle for ship-wide communication. "All hands . . . prepare for warp speed." He paused, then said reluctantly, "We are leaving this area of space because we were apparently exposed to a rare form of radiation. Once we know more about it, Doctor Phlox will inform you as to what steps to take. Archer out."

He braced himself, feeling the deck beneath his feet vibrate as the warp engines powered up. And as the planet Oan disappeared from the viewscreen, replaced by streaming stars, Archer got the unpleasant premonition that the *Enterprise* crew was fleeing something that already held them firmly in its grasp.

The lighting aboard *Enterprise* was muted in deference to Earth's night—as it was in sickbay, where T'Pol watched as a weary-looking Phlox spoke into the companel. Wanderer hovered between them, its radiant field not quite grazing the deck.

"Now that we've established some distance between ourselves and the planet," Phlox said into the bulkhead companel, "I'll be retiring to my quarters if you have no further need of me. I must admit that I'm feeling surprisingly tired. I suspect that the interruption of my annual hibernation cycle must have affected me more than I realize."

Archer's voice filtered back through. "Of course, Doctor. You've earned your rest."

Indeed, T'Pol thought. Phlox had just finished two consecutive shifts of duty, something that was difficult for most humans. Apparently, it was difficult for Phlox as well; shadows had appeared beneath the doctor's deep-set eyes, and his facial skin appeared a shade paler than normal.

"Ensign Cutler has promised to notify me if anything out of the ordinary—" Phlox began, but Archer interrupted him.

"You've done all you can do. You know we'll call you if we need you. Now, go to bed, Doctor."

"With pleasure, Captain." The Denobulan turned his broad, stocky body toward T'Pol and Wanderer, and gave a small nod to both of them—a very human gesture, the Vulcan noted. It had taken her years to master the finer subtleties of Terran non-verbal communication, but Phlox was already a master of it. "Good night, Sub-Commander . . . Wanderer."

"Good night, Doctor," T'Pol said, following the prescribed protocol. Phlox, too, was prey to emotion, just as humans were, though he possessed a Vulcan-keen penchant for observation and investigation. T'Pol heard the heaviness in his tone— one that matched the captain's. She postulated that the cause for their ill-hidden despair was their fear that the crew had in fact been fatally exposed to the rare radiation.

T'Pol could not understand such dread. Some emotions were vaguely understandable, but worry always left her perplexed. Either they were all going to die or they were not, and since there was nothing any of them could do about it, it seemed quite foolish to expend emotional and mental energy thinking about it. If time were limited, would it not be best to spend that time doing more constructive things? Yet, as she watched Phlox exit sickbay, she noted that even his shoulders sagged more than normal: his emotional reaction of concern affected even his posture.

Once the doctor had left, she turned to the entity beside her. The dimmer lighting brought out Wanderer's internal radiance, so that its blue-green glow assisted in illuminating their surroundings. Aesthetically, it was quite pleasing, and reminded T'Pol of the natural phosphorescence of certain of Earth's sea creatures.

"Wanderer," she asked, aware that she was speaking aloud to a creature that could sense her thoughts, and yet finding it quite natural to do so, "would you be interested in taking a tour of the ship, and perhaps examining some of our databases?"

Yes . . .

She moved to the companel. "T'Pol to bridge."

"Archer here. You're lucky you caught me, Sub-Commander. I'm headed off duty."

"Sir, I would like to take Wanderer on a tour of ship, with your permission."

"Of course." Archer himself sounded both tired and frustrated, and was doing little to mask either. "So long as you promise to leave the captain's quarters for another time."

"So noted. T'Pol out."

T'Pol began the tour in sickbay, of course, showing off Phlox's exotic collection of biological creatures used for different diagnostic and medical procedures. Wanderer absorbed most of this in silence; the Vulcan could not tell whether it was bored or fascinated by her explanations. Next, they passed by the research lab where Hoshi—now off duty—had been working.

"This is where we're analyzing the medical logs and data that we recovered from the Oani," T'Pol explained.

Wanderer had but one question: *Are you making progress?*

"So far, no. Apparently, they were quite unaware that they were killed by a form of radiation. Of course, Ensign Sato has not yet finished examining all of the logs."

The tour also included an examination of the main dining room, along with the food replicators; curious, T'Pol asked Wanderer whether it was self-sustaining.

A long pause followed. *Negative*, it replied at last. *We feed on more primitive forms of energy, as you do.*

"You seem to know quite a bit about humanoids."

We have encountered many in our travels.

T'Pol hesitated, then finally asked the question that had persisted in her thoughts throughout the conversation. "If you are somewhat familiar with humanoids, then why can you not use your superior intellect to learn their morphology and physiology? I submit that it might be far easier for you to come up with a cure for the radiation sickness than it would be for us."

You are assuming such a cure exists. Unfortunately, it does not. At least, I am unaware of a method by which humanoids can be completely regenerated, unless you wish to resort to cloning an entirely new body. But that will not save the original. . . .

"Cloning is purposeless in this instance," T'Pol said. "I regret that nothing can be done."

Wanderer made no reply.

At the entry to engineering, Wanderer stopped

and would go no farther. *I cannot enter—to do so would disrupt my field.*

"Very well," T'Pol replied. "Would you like to examine our computer databases? They can give you excellent information on Earth and human culture."

Do the computer databases give information on you?

T'Pol found the question perplexing. "Yes. And I can answer any questions you might have."

You are different from the others on this ship.

"Most of them, with the exception of Doctor Phlox, are human. He is Denobulan. I am a Vulcan."

Why are you with the others? You have a superior intellect, and more ordered thoughts. The others have no mental discipline.

T'Pol reflected that Captain Archer's absence was fortunate; he would find Wanderer's opinions about human beings most irritating.

"Control of the mind and the emotions are prized on my home planet, Vulcan. We practice such control because we were originally a very violent, ill-tempered species."

What made your species change so dramatically?

The memory of the white-haired teacher Sklar surfaced in T'Pol's thoughts, and the day he had posed a question she had not been ready to answer. "We were profoundly influenced by one of our own, a philosopher named Surak. He taught nonviolence toward all beings. For that reason, I do not, as some of the humans do, eat animals. In fact, I recently chose not to wear a weapon to protect myself against more violent species."

Wanderer's form turned a paler shade of blue and enlarged as its energy pattern began to swirl more rapidly; T'Pol wondered whether this was some sort of emotional reaction.

Excellent! Perhaps this is why we found it possible to converse with you. Our culture is much the same: we prize peace above all, and feed only off nonsentient energy sources. We judge violence to be the mark of lower beings. The sudden flow of words stopped abruptly as the entity paused in its communication; then it asked pointedly: *May we use the ship's database to study Vulcan culture?*

"To some extent," T'Pol said. "This is a human, not a Vulcan vessel, and as such, it does not have access to the same amount of information about Vulcan culture."

Had Wanderer been human, she would have judged it to be disappointed. Its sudden surge of brightness dimmed a bit before it replied, *Very well. Then we shall study what information about your culture this ship does have.* It paused. *However, you have not answered my original question: Why have you chosen to be amongst such inferior beings?*

With something very like ruefulness, T'Pol once again reflected that Captain Archer's absence from the tour was fortunate. She answered in the only manner she felt Wanderer would understand.

"I wish—as you do—to observe them."

While T'Pol was leaving Wanderer to its own devices in front of a computer terminal, Archer sat on his bed, legs stretched out, with Porthos in his lap. He had arrived in his quarters to find the beagle completely unsettled about something and insistent on human contact to the point of ignoring his dinner. Now the dog lay sprawled on his back, haunches against Archer's stomach, belly exposed, pink ear flaps spread open, reminding Archer of a bat. As usual, Porthos was overdue for a bath, a situation that usually made the captain (and others) complain about the smell; but today, at least, Archer secretly found *eau de dog* comforting. It smelled like Earth, and home.

What he did not permit himself to think overtly was that, being the small creature that he was, Porthos would probably be first to react to any major dose of radiation.

"What is it, huh, boy?" Archer murmured, scratching Porthos's stomach. One of the dog's lower legs thumped in ecstatic reply against Archer's midsection; he leaned his head back, causing his jowls to fall away from the gums, exposing sharp teeth. "What's the matter?"

"He just knows you're upset, that's what's wrong," Trip Tucker said. He sat in the chair next to the cot, sipping from a shot glass of bourbon, neat.

"Maybe now," Archer said. "He was jittery when I came in. And this dog takes after me. It takes a lot for him to turn his nose up at dinner."

"You weren't exactly a member of the clean-plate club yourself. Sure you don't want a drink?" Trip said, proffering his glass.

"Nah." Archer leaned forward to scratch the pits at the top of Porthos's front legs; the beagle stretched his legs straight upward in appreciation. What Archer wanted, and left unsaid, was to remain alert in case any of his people fell ill.

Trip, as usual, read his mind. "You know, if anybody starts getting sick, there's not a damned thing you or I can do about it, Cap'n."

"Thanks for the encouragement." Archer graced him with a small, bitter smile.

Trip shrugged; his tone held no sympathy. "What *could* any of us do about it? Those people down on that planet couldn't save themselves, and it sounds to me like they were using some pretty whiz-bang technology."

"Yeah, but what about our resident radiation-expert guest? It seems that Wanderer ought to be able to help somehow. That 'he'—it—whatever—knows something it's not telling."

"It was able to warn us," Trip countered. "For all we know, it saved us in time. If it hadn't told us—"

"You're right," Archer admitted. "I just wish—"

"You just wish you could be the perfect captain. Not only protect your crew from harm, but restore those poor dead people to life."

"Exactly," Archer admitted, with a wry grimace that was not quite a grin.

Trip gave a knowing nod. "And *I* wish I could tell you it was gonna be okay—but we just aren't gonna know that for a while."

Archer sighed and opened his mouth to retort, *Could you tell me something just a little less obvious*, when his door buzzed. He scowled faintly. "Now, who would be up at this hour?"

Trip looked at him, and they both said simultaneously, *"T'Pol."*

"Come," Archer said.

The door slid open. To his surprise, Phlox appeared, his normally ruddy flesh pale, all animation fled from his expression. For an instant, he lingered in the doorway, leaning heavily to one side before he sank to his knees.

Archer leaped off the bed without consideration for the dog, who had to scramble out of his way. In an instant, the captain was at Phlox's side, with Trip close behind.

"Captain," Phlox whispered, though the desperation behind the sound made it seem as though he had screamed. As he uttered the word, he shuddered, eyes rolling back in their sockets. "Captain . . ."

Archer barely caught him in time as he pitched face-first toward the deck.

Five

Captain's Starlog, supplemental. Doctor Phlox has fallen ill, apparently with the same illness that afflicted the inhabitants of Oan. Now Enterprise faces a possible plague without the help of her chief medical officer.

IN THE night-dimmed lights of sickbay, Archer stood across from Ensign Cutler while the two of them looked down at the unconscious form of Dr. Phlox. The Denobulan's skin was sunken and sallow; Archer glanced up at the diagnostic readout displayed over Phlox's head and tried to make sense of it.

Nearby, both T'Pol and Wanderer lingered—not, Archer thought grimly, that either of them would be able to help. But just in case, he had summoned them both to sickbay.

"Are you sure that he's suffering from the same disorder that afflicted the Oanis?" Archer asked Cutler.

She let go a sigh. Cutler was young, a bit wide-eyed, with hair that swung easily about her face in a golden-brown arc. She was still unsure of her space legs and most definitely not a doctor. Even as a medic, her experience was limited; but at the time *Enterprise* was launched, it had never occurred to Archer that he might need more than one doctor to tend to the needs of a sixty-person crew. Nor had it occurred to any of the brass who approved *Enterprise*'s launch.

Now the captain could only wonder how they had made such a glaring oversight.

While Cutler struggled valiantly to maintain a professional exterior, Archer knew that the situation was particularly difficult for her: she was closer to Phlox than anyone else on board. A trace of emotion flickered in her brown eyes, but was gone by the time she gazed up at Archer. "It appears so, sir—if only because of the fact that he shows no symptoms other than a gradual ebbing of life functions."

"What can you do for him?" Archer asked.

For an instant, she looked away and down; she did not want to let the captain down by saying

Nothing, Archer understood. Instead, she squared her shoulders and met his gaze again, squarely. "We can help most of his vital organs to keep functioning, sir. So long as there's brain activity . . ."

Total life-support, in other words. "Have you tried standard radiation treatment for Denobulans?"

"No, sir." Cutler brightened a bit. "I'll give that a try."

Archer nodded, knowing full well it would probably do no good; but at least it would allow them some temporary hope. "And go ahead and administer the standard treatment to the rest of the crew. It might help and it certainly can't hurt."

"Aye, sir," Cutler said.

"It'll be quite a task," Archer said. "I'll reassign some crew members to help you."

"Thank you." Cutler paused. "Then let's start right away with you, sir."

Archer waved a hand dismissively, and moved his shoulders slightly in the direction of the doorway. "I'm a little busy right now, Ensign. I think it's important that the rest of the crew—"

"Sir." Cutler drew herself up, and assumed a more commanding air. "This puts me in the position of chief medical officer. And as such, I must point out to you that, unfortunately, the landing party is at highest risk of coming down with radiation sickness. The construction of the ship offers us some protection, sir—but you were down on the planet's surface."

"She's quite right," T'Pol offered; Archer shot her an irritated glance. She lifted her eyebrows in mild surprise and added, "We *were* exposed more than the others, Captain. Therefore, assuming we were exposed sufficiently, we will come down with the malady before the others." She paused a beat. "Denobulans are more susceptible to radiation sickness than humans. It's logical that Doctor Phlox would succumb first."

"Fine." Archer gestured the Vulcan toward Cutler and the diagnostic equipment. "Then I'll order you to go first."

"Vulcans are more resistant to radiation poisoning than humans," T'Pol countered.

Cutler was nodding. "No more arguments, Captain. I'll need you for no more than a minute. . . ." She reached for a medical scanner, waved it over Archer, then went to a different corner and began preparing an injection.

The captain sighed and rolled up his sleeve, but turned to T'Pol. "You next," he said. "While you're waiting, contact Hoshi and Reed, and get them in here ASAP."

Blessedly, T'Pol did not ask for a translation of the acronym, but instead went directly to the companel to comply.

And as Archer felt the cold metal of the hypo

Cutler pressed against his skin, he thought, *For all the good it will do any of us. . . .*

Hoshi was dreaming in Oani.

She often dreamed in other languages; and this night, as on many others, she spoke with perfect fluency, and understood with ease.

She was sitting in the hospital waiting room, where the landing party had witnessed dozens of Oanis sitting patiently in death; but in the dream, the room was entirely empty, save for herself, and Uroqa, and Kano.

They sat beside her in the nacreous mother-of-pearl waiting room, all of them seated cross-legged on the cushioned floor. Both Uroqa and Kano were well, and smiling benevolently at her; as she spoke to them, she gazed from time to time at the wall directly across from them—entirely transparent, revealing a sparkling shore and the ocean, blue-green, with gently rolling waves.

You must not worry about us any more, Uroqa said in his distinctive baritone. *We are safe now. We are happy.*

Kano leaned forward to take his hand—twelve fingers intertwined—and nodded. Her voice was soft, but huskier than Hoshi imagined it might be.

Yes. We are happy. But we are very worried about you.

About me? Hoshi shook her head in surprise. *But I'm not the one who's dead.*

Do you see that? Uroqa asked suddenly, and inclined his broad bronze head toward the transparent wall.

Hoshi followed his gaze. Outside, the glistening white sand had disappeared; the tide had come in, and the water was now beating against the glass at ankle length.

It's only going to keep growing, Kano said calmly, *until it swallows us all.*

The words filled Hoshi with inexplicable dread. She stared at the slowly rising water a time, then back at Kano, delicate and small-framed beside her broad, muscular mate.

What do you mean? Hoshi demanded.

But Kano would not speak again; and Uroqa merely inclined his head again at the glass.

The water rose, and the waves grew, larger and larger, pulling away from the wall with greater and greater force, and then smashing against the glass until Hoshi could see nothing else . . . until at last, they broke through, crashing, sweeping Hoshi and the Oanis up in a tide that pulled incessantly, smothering her, stealing her breath. She screamed, but no sound came. . . .

Except for the *beep* of the companel next to her bunk. She sat bolt upright, struggling to orient herself again to reality and the darkness. She found the blinking light, hit the control, and said—doing her best to keep from gasping—"Sato here."

"Ensign." T'Pol's cool, measured tone was a tonic, making Hoshi instantly alert. "Report to sickbay immediately. T'Pol out."

Hoshi turned on the light and struggled into her uniform, her mind focused on the image of rising waters.

Archer stood waiting in sickbay, keenly aware of the backdrop behind him: that of Ensign Cutler tending Dr. Phlox, unconscious on the diagnostic bed. He also realized how grim his own expression had to have looked—and when Malcolm Reed, and then Hoshi, stepped through the entrance to sickbay within seconds of each other, Archer watched them react.

Reed immediately did a double take at the sight of Phlox down, then grew stone-faced, and stood stiffly at attention; Hoshi simply let her concern show.

For a moment, no one spoke; no one really needed to, Archer realized, but he said what his crewmates already knew.

"Doctor Phlox is in a coma," Archer said. "He's showing the same signs as the Oanis did—slowed pulse and respiration, gradual failure of internal organs. We have to assume it's the radiation Wanderer warned us about." He found himself in the awkward position of suddenly having to clear his throat. "I've ordered standard radiation treatment for everyone in the crew. The landing party first;

because we went down to the planet's surface, we were the most exposed."

As he spoke, Cutler left Phlox's side and moved toward the group, hypos in one hand.

For an instant, Reed looked distinctly uneasy; then he steadied himself, and said easily to Hoshi, "Ladies first."

"Ladies first?" Hoshi looked at him quizzically. "What is that, some sort of British expression?"

"I'm not sure," Reed said. "My grandmother was always saying it so she could be first in the queue." He gestured, and Hoshi shrugged and rolled up her sleeve for Cutler. Within a few seconds, both of them had been inoculated.

"By the way," Archer told them, "I'm going to be waking up the rest of the crew and having them inoculated. It'll go a lot faster if Cutler has volunteers. . . ."

He said it not so much because Cutler needed help, but because he wanted Hoshi and Reed close to sickbay, in case anything happened.

And if anything does happen, what good will it do them? What good did it do Phlox?

"If you don't mind, Captain," Hoshi said, "I was very close to finishing up the Oani medical logs. I'd really like to go ahead with that now." She did not say the obvious—that she was in no mood to return to her quarters, and that if she didn't finish her work now, she might not have the time later. "I just . . . I can't explain it, sir. Even if they didn't know what killed them, I have a feeling that we'll learn something by viewing everything they left. Call it a hunch."

"Go ahead, Ensign. I happen to believe in hunches." Archer gave her a nod; she responded in kind, then left.

"With your permission, sir," Reed said, suddenly military-formal. "I should like to take care of a personal matter. It will only take a moment—"

"Take all the time you need," Archer said gently.

"—at which point I shall return and render whatever assistance I can to Ensign Cutler."

"Go," Archer told him.

For a moment after Reed left, the captain watched the empty doorway; then he sighed as he went to the companel on the wall and pressed the control for shipwide address.

Trip Tucker was sitting on the edge of his bunk, still rubbing his eyes, when the door buzzer sounded. He had been dreaming of the Keys, of diving in the ocean only to suddenly realize he'd been under water for hours without his scuba gear, when the captain's shipwide announcement had wakened him.

"Come," he groaned, then coughed to try to clear the sleep from his voice.

Malcolm Reed entered and stood in the open doorway, in uniform, hair neatly groomed.

"Malcolm," Trip said. "You're looking entirely too sheveled."

Reed drew his head back, confused; he was deeply preoccupied, and responded with no humor whatsoever. "Entirely too . . . what?"

"Sheveled. As opposed to dis-." Trip paused to squint at him more closely. "How the hell did you get out of bed and into uniform so fast?"

"Oh." Reed stepped forward, permitting the door to close behind him. "I've . . . I've been up for a while. That's what I've come to talk to you about, Commander."

"Well, can it wait? There's this little matter of the captain ordering everyone to sickbay. . . ." Trip forced himself onto his feet, pulled a uniform off the nearest rung, and began pulling it on.

"Yes, I know. I was just there." Reed paused, then launched into speech with swift urgency. "Look, Trip, I know that when we were trapped on the shuttlepod and we thought the *Enterprise* was destroyed and that we were goners, you overheard me making a will. . . ."

"Oh, for God's sake," Trip said. "Is that what this is all about? There you go being premature again. . . ." He hopped on one foot, trying to pull on a boot. "Sometimes, Lieutenant, you can be a bit—overly dramatic."

Reed's lean face composed itself into somber, dignified lines. "I'm not being dramatic," he said evenly. "Those of us who went down onto the planet's surface were exposed more than those who remained on the ship. I need for you to know—"

One boot on, Tucker stopped hopping. "Are you sure about that?"

"Yes. And I want to speak to you about my will."

"Well, why don't you just make a tape? Why tell me?" Tucker pulled the other boot on, then straightened to face his friend.

"Because I may not have time."

"Malcolm . . ." Trip groaned, in his *will you please quit being so dramatic* tone.

"Doctor Phlox is in a coma," Reed said. "I'll make a tape, if there's time, but I just wanted to make sure I talked to you first."

"Ah, hell." Trip sat, deflated. "I'm sorry to hear that. Are they sure it's the—"

"It's the radiation, yes." Reed paused. "I want you to have everything."

"What?"

"You heard me. Everything."

"But . . . but what happened to all those girl-friends?" Trip asked. Reed's generosity left him feeling secretly embarrassed by the implication of affection. "All the women? Your parents? Your sister?" He rose. "Look, I've got to report to sick-bay. Let's talk about this later. . . ."

"There might not be a later," Reed intoned, as Tucker walked past him and out the door.

"Look," Trip said, as Reed caught up with him quickly in the corridor, which was already filled with bleary-eyed personnel headed for the turbo-lift. "Keep your will the way it was. After all, *I've* been exposed to the radiation, too." He kept his tone light, matter-of-fact. "So if we're both goners, there's no point in your going to the trouble."

Reed ignored him. "There's some property in the Caymans. Quite a large agricultural spread in Argentina. And a flat in Knightsbridge . . ."

Trip felt a muscle in his jaw begin to twitch. He was tired, and although the news about Phlox was upsetting, he could not take any talk of death seriously. They would find a solution, just as they'd found a solution for every other life-threatening dilemma they'd faced since *Enterprise* had first launched. An innate optimist, Trip simply could not conceive of the crew succumbing to the malady that had claimed the Oanis. "Knock it off, Lieutenant," he said shortly. "We've got better things to do right now than worry about your real-estate holdings."

As they stepped onto the turbolift, crowded with groggy officers, Reed stepped beside him. Sotto voce, in a voice barely loud enough for the others to hear—but loud enough to embarrass Trip—Reed said, "I'm quite serious, Commander Tucker. I've never been one for making friends, but I've come to consider you—"

"Knock it *off*," Tucker repeated, this time with

more irritation in his tone than he actually felt. Now, in front of other crewmates, was not the time to discuss their growing friendship—and again, he felt sure that Reed was overreacting. Staring straight ahead at the turbolift doors, he said, "That's an order, Lieutenant."

Reed broke off in midsentence. He said not another word—reason enough for Trip to glance sidewise at him and see the stony expression that had spread across his features.

Damn, Trip thought. He had not meant to hurt Malcolm's feelings—but he also was in no mood to indulge thoughts of death. If *Enterprise* really was facing a crisis, then it was better that they all be a little angry than resigned or full of fear.

They made their way in silence all the way to sickbay.

Back in her lab, Hoshi did her best to ignore the constant march of people in the corridor, headed to and from sickbay. It wasn't easy trying to blot out the image of Dr. Phlox lying unconscious on the diagnostic bed—it kept mixing with the image of Kano's corpse, temporarily animated from within by the blue-green energy creature— but Hoshi finally forced herself to concentrate on the one image in front of her: that of Uroqa, making yet another entry in his log.

This time, the Oani's expression was animated, hopeful, his large eyes wide. Hoshi listened carefully, able to understand the entry completely without having to listen to it twice.

A stranger has come to our world: a stranger who brings hope. He has come alone, from the planet [here Hoshi made a note in phonetic transcription of the planet name, which sounded like Shikeda], *and he says that his people know of this illness. The other doctors are currently interviewing him, and it is our hope that we will soon find the answer to our woes.*

Hoshi listened without pause, eager for the next entry. Were there other aliens in this area of the space who were familiar with this type of radiation illness—and did they perhaps know of a solution that, while it had come too late for the Oanis, might help the *Enterprise* crew?

The next image tore at her heart. As eager and excited as Uroqa had been, now he was completely overwhelmed with despair; the strong shoulders beneath the gauzy white tunic sagged beneath the weight of an intolerable burden.

For whoever comes after us, he said sadly, his once vibrant voice reduced almost to a whisper, *a warning. The traveler from Shikeda says that the cause of our illness is indeed a microbe, unlike any other with which we are familiar. His own people have suffered and died from it.*

"A microbe!" Hoshi actually stood up, her gaze still fixed on Uroqa's image on the viewer. "No, no, he's wrong! No wonder . . ."

She trailed off as Uroqa bowed his head in sorrow, then looked up steadily at the screen and continued. *It is a life-form, as we are; the traveler confirms that it is capable of evolution, even as he offers us a cure. But we cannot kill it—which we would have to do if we are to survive.* He paused. *We must accept our fate. As a people we lived in peace; so it is we shall die in peace. . . .*

"No!" Hoshi shouted, unaware that she had raised her voice, not caring that she was arguing with the recorded image of a man who had been dead some days. "No, it isn't fair. How can you let yourself die like that? How can you simply give up?"

The image of Uroqa faded, only to be replaced by his final entry, but Hoshi could bear no more. She froze the image, then rose and hurried to the companel.

"Sato to Captain Archer . . ."

No response from the captain's quarters. Hoshi tried the bridge next.

"Archer here."

"Captain, before the Oanis died someone from the planet Shikeda visited them and told them they died from a microbe too small for their instruments to detect. It was against the Oanis' belief to kill any life-form—even one so tiny—so they let themselves die. But this traveler had a cure!"

She could hear the captain's slow release of breath as he registered the information. After a brief pause, he said, "I'll meet you down in sickbay. I think we need to have a little chat with Wanderer about this."

At that same moment in sickbay, Trip Tucker stood flanked by Ensign Cutler and Malcolm Reed. The three of them, along with a former civilian medic who'd joined Starfleet and switched to maintenance, stood with their backs to a counter covered with medical supplies.

Trip was good at giving injections; he had a strong stomach for that sort of thing, and his hand was steady, so once he received his own antiradiation treatment, it only made sense for him to volunteer to help Cutler. With sixty people to inject, it'd take her a few hours alone; and since time was of the essence, Trip figured he'd help out. It was easy work.

Of course, you'd never know it from watching Reed: although he was doing his best to maintain a stoic pose, he wound up gritting his teeth and flinching each time he pressed down on the hypo. Trip pitied his patients—and pitied himself, too, because he had to fight the urge to grin at Reed's squeamishness.

But at least the guy was out here helping. And within a matter of fifteen minutes, they'd managed to treat more than half the crew. The captain would be pleased—assuming, of course, that the captain really felt that injections would do any good. Trip doubted they would, but he also felt it was better to be on the safe side and try everything.

Beside him, Reed pressed down on the hypo and, at the same time, let go a little groan; this time, Trip couldn't help himself. As another crew member stepped up to receive an injection from him, one corner of his mouth quirked upward in a minuscule grin as he murmured out of the other corner, on the side toward Reed, "Careful. Don't want to scare the patients. Of course, one look at that ugly mug of yours and—"

"Help me," Reed said.

He enunciated it quite clearly, in that formal British accent of his, without any sort of inflection at all; Trip heard no fear in his tone, no dismay, no teasing—which is what he at first thought it was.

But it was no joke. The male ensign who stood in front of Reed cried out.

"Hey! Watch that hypo!"

Trip Tucker became immediately aware, in his peripheral vision, of Reed lurching backward, against the counter. He turned.

"Malcolm?"

Reed's eyes were wide and unfocused, as though he were staring at something just past the bulkhead across from him. Beneath the five-o'clock shadow of beard on his chin and cheeks, his skin had grown deathly pale.

Without looking at Tucker, Reed began to slide down, back against the counter.

On pure instinct, Tucker dropped the readied hypo in his hand—it went clattering across the metal deck—turned, and caught his friend before Reed sagged all the way to the floor. Cutler turned, and gave a short cry as well; the crew members standing in line scattered in their efforts to move out of the way.

"You're all right, buddy," Trip said, which struck him as a perfectly ridiculous thing to say. Reed was clearly anything but: by this time, his eyes were rolling back in his head, and his mouth was working, but now only the very faintest sound came out.

Trip leaned his head down to listen.

"*. . . what I said . . . remember . . .*"

"Don't worry, Malcolm," Trip said. "I won't forget." As he spoke, Reed's eyes closed, and he let go a long, sighing breath, then went perfectly limp in Trip's arms.

Cutler rushed to him and did a quick scan.

"He's fainted," she said. "He's fine."

"*What?*" Trip asked, suddenly disgusted with himself for thinking his friend was dying.

Cutler shrugged. "He's fainted. I've seen this happen. People who don't seem the least bit funny around medical stuff, and all the sudden, when you give them an injection, they just keel over. . . ."

"Ooh." Reed's eyelids fluttered. "What's happened?" He stirred in Trip's arms. "Was it the radiation?"

Trip less-than-gently pushed his friend up and onto his feet; Reed swayed slightly while Cutler fetched a different hypo and administered it.

"There," Cutler announced. "That'll help."

"What happened?" Reed asked again.

"You passed out," Trip said flatly. "Why didn't you say you got light-headed around medical stuff?"

Reed sniffed; clearly, Cutler's hypo made him feel well enough to be insulted. "I *don't*. I just suddenly felt weak."

Cutler's smile was small and diplomatic. "Well, just in case, I'm ordering you to your quarters to rest, Lieutenant."

"Very well," Reed said stiffly. He brushed himself off a bit, then moved toward the exit. Before he reached it, he turned and said, "Of course, should you be needing for help—"

"You'll be the last one we call," Trip said archly. He watched, shaking his head in amusement and disgust, as his friend made his way down the corridor.

Once in his quarters, Reed lay down with a sudden delicious sense of exhaustion, as if he wanted to sleep forever and never waken.

He fell onto his bunk, all sense of embarrassment at having fainted in sickbay forgotten. He usually *wasn't* all that squeamish about things medical, and the fact that he'd passed out alarmed him somewhat . . . but at the moment, he no longer cared. He only craved rest.

And at the instant he lay down, he fell into a strange waking dream. The oceans of Oan, turquoise and beautiful, rolled over him, sweeping him away on their currents, and he opened his lungs to them and breathed in the cool, sunlit water . . .

And realized he was drowning. Bone-deep weakness came over him, saturated him, and he struggled against it, mentally clawing like a drowning man fights the water. He opened his eyes, and with his last fragment of strength, painfully dragged himself from his bed, and pressed his body to the bulkhead. His finger trembled as it pressed the companel control.

"Sickbay. Cutler here."

"Help me," Reed whispered, then slid down the length of the wall to the deck, and oblivion.

Six

IN THE LAB just outside sickbay, surrounded by de-contaminated data retrieved from the Oani planet's surface, Archer stood beside Hoshi and let her explain to T'Pol—accompanied, as always, by the nebulous Wanderer—what she had learned from the medical logs of one of the perished doctors.

Archer was angry—angry at the situation, angry at T'Pol for taking the alien on an extended tour of the vessel even though he had given permission for her to do so, angry with a vengeance at Wanderer. He remained unconvinced that his anger was entirely rational—at least some of it had to do with the fact that Phlox was stricken and apparently dying (he hadn't yet checked in with Cutler on the doctor's current status), and with the specter of the entire *Enterprise* crew following suit. *It has nothing to do with the fact that I haven't gotten any sleep. . . .*

But for a very rational reason, he was downright furious that Wanderer hadn't mentioned anyone from the planet Shikeda.

T'Pol listened impassively to Hoshi's tale, glanced briefly at the shimmering creature beside her, then said, "It's true that Wanderer passed by the planet Oan. But Wanderer says that this other traveler was quite mistaken in terms of what destroyed the Oanis. Wanderer says that it was radiation."

"What if it's wrong?" Hoshi countered hotly, a split second before Archer could demand the very same thing.

At least I'm not the only one who's mad. "Exactly." Archer crossed his arms over his chest and stared expectantly at the energy column, as if waiting for it to address him directly. "How can Wanderer be so certain?"

T'Pol's eyes widened ever so slightly; her lips parted an instant before she finally said, in a tone that struck Archer as being cooler than usual, "Captain. Wanderer is an extremely intelligent, very highly evolved being. I doubt it is mistaken."

"As opposed to a puny humanoid with a body?" Archer said, allowing some of the anger through in his tone. "Wanderer may be evolved, and more intelligent than we are, but that doesn't make it entirely incapable of mistakes. Of course, I'll apologize at once if Wanderer can show us *how* it knows there is no microbe involved."

T'Pol glanced at the creature beside her; after a space of silence, she spoke again. "The problem here is the same as with the radiation. Our detection devices are very primitive. Wanderer could show us the radiation if only we were more advanced. . . ."

Archer turned on her with vehemence. "You know, you'd think you wanted to do something other than come up with explanations as to why we all have to die. Don't you want to live, Sub-Commander?"

"Of course," T'Pol said, so unruffled and composed in the face of Archer's frustration that he became even more irritated. "Like most humanoids, I possess an inborn survival instinct." She paused. "But I have been trained not to let emotion prevent me from accepting the inevitable."

The comment rankled, but Archer forced himself to cool his tone. "Well, then, let's approach this more rationally. What proof do you have that Wanderer is correct about the radiation?"

Again, T'Pol turned her head and tilted it upward to look at her amorphous companion; its ocean-blue glow reflected off her face, bringing out the faint greenish highlights in her complexion. "I have none," she stated flatly.

"And what proof do you have that the alien

from Shikeda was wrong in saying that the Oani were killed by a microbe too small for their instruments to detect?"

"Again, none." T'Pol frowned slightly. "However, Captain, if I were forced to calculate the odds of which alien is correct—"

Archer lifted an index finger for silence. "Odds don't matter. This is survival, remember? I'll take any chance, however remote, that we can get. Ask Wanderer where the Shikeda traveler is. We need to find him. And if we can't find him, then let's find his planet. What if he's right? What if his civilization is more advanced than Wanderer's, and can detect a microbe that Wanderer doesn't know is there?"

Once more, T'Pol turned and silently addressed herself to Wanderer; while still looking at its fluctuating energy fields, she said, "Wanderer takes no offense, Captain."

I should hope not, Archer almost said, but held his tongue and let the Vulcan finish.

"Wanderer agrees to try to find the Shikedan. It says that he—the Shikedan traveler and his ship—would, by this time, be more distant from *Enterprise* than his home planet is. Do you prefer to go to the planet, since it is closer?"

Archer thought of the Oani tissue samples in sickbay. "Of course. And the sooner we get there, the better. I want *Enterprise* headed there at maximum warp."

"Very well," T'Pol said. "Wanderer will transmit a course to Ensign Mayweather's station as soon as it has ascertained the location of the Shikedan's ship."

"Thank you," Archer said to Wanderer—though he meant it not in the least. And then he headed to sickbay proper, to check on Dr. Phlox.

After giving orders to the helm to make haste for the planet Shikeda, Archer arrived in sickbay just in time to see Trip Tucker administer the last injection to the last crew member, then set down his hypo. Behind him, Ensign Cutler was bent over a diagnostic bed—Phlox, the captain assumed. He stepped up to Trip, expecting the engineer to ask immediately why the ship had gone into warp.

But Tucker seemed not even to notice something that normally would have him chomping to get to his post in order to nurse his precious warp engines. Instead, he looked up at the captain with a gaze that seemed slightly lost.

"Trip," Archer said softly, reaching out to catch his chief engineer's upper arm. "You okay?"

Physically, Tucker looked fine—not even tired, even though he'd jumped out of bed in the middle of the night then volunteered to help Cutler inoculate the crew against radiation sickness. That was Trip: always ready for action, always the last one still on his feet. But Trip's expression was haunted.

"Malcolm," he said, and even before he turned to look at Cutler behind him, Archer felt dread settle into the pit of his stomach, then spread slowly outward over the rest of him.

There, on the diagnostic beds, were *two* patients now: Phlox, his eyes and cheeks looking even more sunken than before, and Malcolm Reed, pale and still. Archer did not have to look at the overhead scanners to know what was happening to the two men: life was all too obviously ebbing from them.

He took the stricken Trip's elbow and guided him over toward Cutler and her patients. She was bent over Reed at the moment, administering a hypo, and she looked intently at the results as she straightened. One indicator on Reed's overhead scanner moved up very slightly; the others stayed put.

"I just can't seem to do anything for him." She faced the captain, her voice filled with the same frustration and anger Archer had experienced when questioning Wanderer.

"How's Phlox?" Archer asked softly, and braced himself for the obvious answer.

She shook her head. "He's deteriorating and I can't stop it."

Archer let a long moment of silence pass between the three of them before speaking again. "How long?"

Her eyes narrowed slightly with pain. "A day, if

he continues declining at the same rate. With Reed, I don't know yet."

Archer gave a single, unhappy nod. "There might be hope. Hoshi just reported that a traveler from another planet visited the Oanis and apparently had a cure, which they refused for philosophical reasons. Wanderer is helping us track down that traveler right now." He made the situation sound better than it actually was; it was important for Cutler, at least, to have hope if she was to maintain sanity here in sickbay.

"Good," Cutler said, but the enthusiasm in her tone was muted. "Any idea how long that'll take?"

"I'll check on it and get back to you," Archer promised. "Trip, we need to take a little stop by engineering. I need you to coax everything you can from those engines."

The captain made good on his promise; Wanderer predicted that the planet Shikeda was reachable within twenty hours, so long as *Enterprise* was not forced to slow her speed. The creature was now happily settled in front of the computers in the lab near sickbay. Once Cutler was informed and warp four-point-five reached, Archer dragged Trip Tucker with him to his quarters and sat him down, once again with a glass of bourbon.

Tucker sighed. "Isn't this where our evening started?"

"Not quite," Archer said darkly, legs stretched out in front of him on the bed. On the deck between him and Trip, Porthos paced nervously and whined.

"I know, boy," Archer said. "You just wish I would settle down and get to sleep, so you'd know everything was back to normal. But it isn't. Come on." He patted the space between his legs; Porthos immediately jumped up and curled himself into a canine crescent, chin on Archer's thigh, worried gaze on his master's face.

"I just feel like such a damned heel," Trip said finally, the first normal Trip-sounding noise he'd made since they were in sickbay.

"Why should you feel like a heel? Cutler said you caught Malcolm before he hit the deck."

"Yeah, but he tried . . ." Trip broke off, his voice suspiciously wavering; he coughed, then threw back his head and took a stiff belt of bourbon. Then he sighed deeply, and the resulting alcohol breeze made Archer wince ever so slightly. "Aw, heck, he tried to tell me he was changing his will and leaving everything to me. Then he fainted in sickbay, and I made fun of him. . . ."

Archer decided that the best way to diffuse the tension was to add a little hard-boiled levity. "Yeah? And did you ask him what would happen to the family jewels when *you* croaked?"

It worked; Tucker's lips curved in a faint ghost of a grin. "Depraved minds think alike. That's exactly what I pointed out to him, Captain. But he was damned determined." He let go a huff of air, half out of humor, half out of pain. "For a Starfleet stiff, he's pretty well off. Seems he's got some property in the Cayman Islands, a huge spread in Argentina, a place in a hoity-toity London neighborhood . . ."

"All you have to do is survive, Commander," Archer told him. "Who knows? Behave yourself, and I might leave that little condo on Kauai to you. . . . You could come out of this one ahead. And of course, there's Porthos, here." He stroked the dog's smooth, warm head.

"Keep the condo," Tucker said. "I'll fight with Hoshi over the dog. I could use a little companionship."

"That's what the condo on Kauai's for," Archer said, and they both shared a feeble laugh. It faded quickly; Archer reached for the shelf beside the bed, where he'd left the picture of his father with Zefram Cochrane. He held the picture in one palm and gazed at it.

"Who's that?" Trip asked.

"My dad." Archer stared at the image a moment before he spoke. It occurred to him with resounding simplicity that, despite the occasional loneliness of the life he'd chosen, he was irrevocably *happy*—glad every morning when he woke to realize where he was and what he was doing; grateful every night for the same when he went to sleep.

That very fact made the thought of his own death less terrifying, even if he could never reconcile himself to the thought of losing a single crew member. "You know, I've really got it made. I've gotten everything I wanted out of life: a starship, a loyal crew, a life full of experiences I never dreamed of . . ."

"A condo on Kauai," Trip countered archly. "Captain, don't get morbid on me."

Archer sighed and straightened, carefully so as not to disturb the now-napping Porthos. "Trip, you know I've got to. The situation isn't good."

All pretense of good humor fled Tucker's features; they sagged downward as he set his glass down on Archer's desk and said, darkly, "I know."

"We're not even sure the Shikedans can help us. And twenty hours to get there—that's a long time." He did not add, *A lot of people can die in that time.* When Trip looked away and failed to reply, Archer continued. "There are a few things we need to talk about—as captain and commander."

Tucker straightened and faced him. "Yes, sir."

"Let's assume I'm out of commission. The first situation is that T'Pol will assume command. I want to be sure that this ship gets in touch with the Shikedans. I'm leaving taped orders to that effect; and if she doesn't comply, then I'm ordering you to take command and fulfill those orders. We've got to be certain this isn't a microbe."

It was tantamount to mutiny for Trip to override T'Pol—but he didn't even flinch at the thought. "You've got it, Captain."

"Second thing: I want to be sure that, if this is a microbe, it doesn't spread."

"Understood. I'll make sure strict quarantine is maintained until we're sure."

"Good." Archer paused, then absently stroked Porthos's head; the dog opened one eye and glared balefully at him for disturbing his slumber. "Third: If we *do* lose a lot of crew . . ." He sighed, casting about for the right words. "If more than just the landing party is affected . . ."

Trip read his mind. "You don't want the Vulcans using this as an excuse to scrap the mission."

It was a reasonable worry; while T'Pol might now thoroughly support the right of humans to explore space without their big Vulcan brother watching their every move, the same could still not be said for her superior, Ambassador Soval. Soval would be first to claim that any disaster involving *Enterprise* was proof that she should be recalled home.

Archer nodded grimly, glancing down at the image of his father and promising silently, *Never.*

He looked up to see Trip studying the captain's expression, and reading it loud and clear.

"I'll stop it, sir," Tucker vowed. He did not qualify the statement by saying, *If at all possible,* an omission Archer noted and appreciated. "You have my word."

"Good," Archer said. He lifted Porthos into his arms and stood. "Now let's see if we can't get a few hours' sleep before the next shift."

Trip set down his partially drunk glass of bourbon and rose stiffly, stretching as he did so. "God knows I could use some."

"Me, too," Archer said. "See you in the morning."

As he stood in the doorway, Trip shot him a look that said, *I'll take that as a promise.* "See you in the morning, Captain."

Exhausted and bleary-eyed, Hoshi worked in her small laboratory near sickbay, which she now shared—most uncomfortably—with Wanderer. T'Pol had gone to the bridge to take over the conn, leaving the entity to scan *Enterprise*'s databases, presumably in order to learn more about human and Vulcan culture.

"Hello," Hoshi had greeted the semitransparent column of blue-green swirls when it had first entered the laboratory. The presence of the energy being made Hoshi nervous, perhaps because of pure human prejudice: it just seemed unnatural that a conscious creature should not possess a body. Or perhaps her discomfort was due to the fact that her whole life was centered around communicating with other species—and here was one species that she could not communicate with.

Most of all, perhaps a part of her could not forgive Wanderer for desecrating Kano's body.

Yet at the same time, it had seemed rude not to acknowledge its presence here in her lab—even if she didn't know whether it understood her or not. "I'm just finishing up my work on Oani logs," she had told it.

Maybe the column had tried to respond: it deepened in color, grew a bit more opaque—*like the ocean before a storm,* Hoshi had thought, then turned away from the creature swiftly, before it could see the involuntary dismay in her expression. The thought had caused her to remember the disturbing dream of the night before, of Kano and Uroqa looking calmly at the waves pounding against the window.

It's only going to keep growing until it swallows us all.

Hoshi had shuddered at the memory. It hadn't helped her nerves any to learn that Malcolm Reed, who had just been looking perfectly normal as he stood next to her in sickbay, had later collapsed. It broke her heart even more than the thought of viewing Uroqa's last entry: she'd always liked Malcolm, more than she let on. There was something endearing about his awkard military stiffness and his pretense of being a suave ladies' man, when in fact he was anything but.

And now, only she, the captain, and T'Pol were left from the original landing party. T'Pol would definitely be the last to succumb to any sickness—God help the microbe or radioactive particle that tried to pierce that Vulcan hide. Which left Hoshi wondering whether her tiredness was due to the fact that she hadn't slept all night . . . or was due to some more sinister cause.

Hoshi leaned over the hooded viewer and finally steeled herself to watch the final log entry. In terms of discovering a solution to *Enterprise*'s medical dilemma, there seemed little point in viewing the entry: either Wanderer was correct about radiation poisoning, or the mysterious Shikedan traveler was correct about a microbe. But as a linguist, each entry provided Hoshi with more information on the (unfortunately now dead) Oani language; and as a scientist, she could not be one-hundred-percent certain that some sort of useful medical data might not come out of this last recording.

As a caring being, she felt obliged to see Uroqa's sad story through to the very end.

Hoshi drew a breath and pressed the control that put Uroqua's frozen image back in motion. As always, he began the log entry by identifying himself and giving the date and time, and mentioning any historical significance either of them had. This last entry was the birthdate of one of the Oani's most technologically progressive leaders, one born many centuries earlier, who had discovered how to effectively eliminate a great deal of the atmospheric pollution left behind by previous generations.

She was surprised to see Uroqa still physically strong, although emotionally drained by the tragedy surrounding him.

All dying or dead, he intoned, his once-forceful voice reduced to a murmur. *It will not be long for Kano now, and so I yearn for my own death to come quickly.*

It is so quiet here. The voices all are stilled, except my own. And I will be silent soon: I die so another creature, one too small for my eyes to see, might live. Yet its effects on my body will lead to its own destruction.

Is there meaning in this? I see none. Only darkness . . .

He paused, and Hoshi pressed a control, freezing his image; her eyes were filled with tears, and she wanted to regain control of herself—for some reason embarrassed that Wanderer might see her weep over the death of this stranger, this alien.

And then she felt suddenly disgusted with herself for caring what anyone else thought. Why shouldn't she weep? Why shouldn't she feel compassion for the passing of this caring man and his wonderful civilization?

Hoshi glanced over her shoulder: to her relief, Wanderer had vanished, apparently having finished its scan of the *Enterprise* computers.

She pressed the control again, then let the image play. But Uroqa had gone silent, gazing into the screen with an expression of eloquent sorrow; and then he turned his head and looked at something—someone—off-camera. His features did not shift, though his gaze was one of recognition.

I am sorry your help has been all for nothing, he said.

His intonation was irregular—not, Hoshi noted, the same he used when he was speaking to Kano, or making a log entry, but the one he used when he murmured something to himself. Someone had just entered, but for some reason Uroqa did not speak directly to them.

And then, not as visible on his deep bronze features, but clearly visible on his stark white tunic, shone a blue-green glow: oceanic, roiling, like the rippling of a strong current. It neared Uroqa; closer and closer it came, until in its deep turquoise light he let go a gasp so deep it seemed all the air had been forced from his lungs.

You, he hissed, with such venom, such fury and bitterness, that even Hoshi recoiled, and he rose up from his chair—staggering, struggling against a sudden weakness. There came the sounds of his uneven footfall as he used the last of his strength to go to his wife's side. . . .

Then there was nothing but pale walls tinted with the sea-blue glow.

Seething, body taut, Hoshi punched the control on the nearest companel, and turned, ready to make the accusation.

Wanderer was, of course, still gone.

But in its place at the computer console, Kano—Uroqa's dead mate—stood, her white tunic draped about her erect, stiff body like a shroud. Her dulled eyes were open, but unfocused, and her arms stretched out over the keyboard while her fingers punched the controls with the preternatural speed and grace of a pianist-prodigy.

Dear God, this isn't happening, Hoshi tried to say, but her tongue, her lips were frozen with disbelief and horror. Somehow, her limbs still worked, and she took a step toward the impossible.

Kano lifted her fingers and paused, head tilting, sensing an intruder's approach.

At once, the Oani woman dropped to the floor with the dreadful limpness of death, all animation fled from her corpse, white gauze draping over her bronze skin and fluttering out onto the deck about her.

In her place at the console, Wanderer, a neatly condensed column of energy, remained.

Hoshi recoiled. But the weakness—one so

draining, so powerfully intense it verged on anguish and made her long for an end, for death—overtook her so swiftly so that she could manage only one whispered word as her eyesight dimmed, replaced by an all-enveloping blue-green glow:

"*You . . .*"

Seven

"You . . ."

The word woke Archer from a deep, dreamless sleep. For a few seconds he stared, dazed and disoriented, face still crushed against his pillow, at the companel where the sound had originated.

He blinked. Beside him, curled in a horseshoe shape, Porthos snored, having ignored the rule—most definitely spoken—that he was to spend all nights in his own bed.

Archer pushed himself up on one elbow and cleared his throat; a glance at the chronometer confirmed he'd gotten less than two hours' sleep, which explained the mental fuzziness. He fought to shake it off, to replay the single word in his mind to try to determine who had uttered it.

"Archer here," he croaked, and cleared his

throat again. On the next try, his voice sounded more like his own. "Hoshi?"

Silence, but Archer's hearing was sharp. The channel was still open.

"Hoshi, come in."

Still no response. Archer sat, then stood, all the while feeling an increasing sense of alarm. "Ensign Sato, report."

At this point, he did not expect a reply. He cut off the channel himself, and instead opened one to sickbay.

"Cutler here." She sounded wearier than Archer felt.

"Ensign, send someone down to Hoshi Sato's lab at once. She tried to contact me, but I'm not able to raise her now. I'm concerned . . ."

"I'll get someone down there right away, sir." She paused. "We've got some strange problems down here, Captain."

"Strange?"

"An Oani corpse has disappeared, sir."

"*What?*"

"That was my reaction, too, Captain. It's not like we misplaced it—sickbay's too small for that. It was in its stasis container when Lieutenant Reed collapsed, sir, and now, it's . . . gone."

"Ensign, we can't have any breach of containment like that. That's inexcusable."

"Yes, sir."

He could practically hear Cutler flush with em-

131

barrassment on the other end. "Well, recruit someone to deal with it. Find that corpse, Ensign. But first, someone needs to go check on Ensign Sato."

"Yes, sir."

Archer punched the control and on instinct began to head for the door—then stopped himself. The problem with the corpse he had dismissed as an oversight—Cutler was overstressed, overworked, overwhelmed . . . she had moved the Oani and no doubt forgotten about it. The captain had thought to head for sickbay, to check on Hoshi himself, then to the bridge since it was only an hour before his regular shift began anyway. But his brain, fatigued and still hovering near the half-waking, half-dreaming state where insight dwelled, seized on a sudden idea, halting his body in midstep.

"*You . . .*"

Hoshi had been speaking to someone else, not directly to Archer. She had opened the channel, but she had been interrupted before she had been able to address the captain. And her tone had been . . . not normal. Archer paused, remembering the emotions carried on that single word. She had sounded angry. Accusatory.

There was only one other person—*creature*, Archer corrected himself—working in the lab with her.

Wanderer.

Revelation born of pure instinct overtook him, and with it, a sense of dread that left him physically chilled—not out of personal fear, but out of the sickening realization that he had voluntarily been playing host to the very entity that was killing his people, that had killed all the Oanis, and had done so without leaving a trace.

He headed back to the companel and pressed the control, now beyond awake, all tiredness forgotten; he could barely hold himself still for the millisecond before Cutler replied, again in a tone that was beyond exhausted.

His words came rapid-fire. "Cutler, I want to know the instant you find Hoshi how she's doing—and I need to know whether Wanderer is still in the lab with her. If your medic doesn't return at once, I want to know about that, too. I don't want anyone else being alone with Wanderer—"

There was a dazed pause as Cutler struggled to digest everything; then she said, her tone a bit more alert, "Hold on, Captain. The orderly's coming back right now—you're right, he's carrying Hoshi. She's unconscious . . ."

"Ask him. Ask him whether Wanderer's still in that lab."

Another pause; Archer listened as Cutler repeated the question, and heard the negative reply even before she could relay it to him.

"I heard, Ensign. I want no one going near that

lab anyway. Wait in sickbay until you receive further orders from me. Archer out." He pressed another toggle. "Archer to bridge."

"T'Pol here."

"Sub-Commander. I need to talk to you—in private, where Wanderer can't hear us. Is there any possible way for us to do that?"

Archer entered engineering to find Trip Tucker already on duty—like his captain, an hour before his shift. T'Pol was already there and waiting, arms folded, looking as fresh as if she had just risen instead of spending the last two nights without sleeping. Trip looked haggard, but intrigued—even more so after one glance at the captain's taut expression.

"Wanderer refuses to enter engineering," T'Pol explained, the instant Archer stepped through the doorway. "Apparently, something about the warp engines disrupts its energy patterns."

The information gave Archer yet another reason to find the hum of engines and the vibration beneath his feet even more reassuring. "There's a problem with our new friend," Archer said.

T'Pol tilted her head expectantly.

"I believe the cause of the mysterious deaths is Wanderer," the captain continued. "Hoshi tried to contact me from the lab. She wasn't able to finish what she was trying to say. All she managed to say was 'You . . .'" He gave it the same accusatory intonation he remembered hearing.

"Son of a . . ." Trip let go a breath of surprise; the emotion was soon replaced by anger. His eyes narrowed. "No wonder it gave us that cock-and-bull story about radiation we couldn't detect."

"For some reason, it's killing us," Archer said, with vehement conviction. "Just like it killed the Oanis."

T'Pol regarded him with cold-blooded disbelief. "What proof do you have, Captain? Surely you don't consider Hoshi's attempt to contact you as conclusive."

"How else do you explain it?" Archer demanded, even though he understood her position completely. He *had* no direct proof, other than an unshakable belief.

But the Vulcan was equally immovable. "Wanderer is a pacifist, Captain. It explained to me how it does not believe in killing."

"How do you know it doesn't believe in lying?" Trip shot at her; his barb drew her sharp glance.

"Its beliefs are very similar to those of Vulcans," T'Pol insisted. "It is quite evolved. And it would be most disgusted by your accusations. What possible reason would it have to kill humanoids?"

For that, Archer had no answer; but Trip was all engineer when he replied, "It consists of energy, right?"

T'Pol allowed a single, tight nod.

"Well, how does it renew itself? What's its energy source, Sub-Commander? How does it *feed?*" Archer felt his lips twist with revulsion.

"It has not discussed that with me," T'Pol admitted. "But it agreed with me at length that it was against violence of all forms. It specifically stated it was against killing sentient beings." She paused. "If it was lying, why did it not destroy us all when it first came aboard?"

"Maybe it was full," Archer said. He was not entirely joking.

"And maybe it's amusing itself in the interim," Trip added. "Going along for the ride until it works up an appetite." A sudden thought alarmed him; he glanced swiftly at Archer. "It's studying our computer database, right? Then it's going to be able to locate Earth and Vulcan and other inhabited planets. . . ."

"We've got to stop it," Archer said. "No matter what it takes."

As the captain expected, T'Pol protested at once. "Sir, how can you even discuss such a prospect without proof that Wanderer is indeed a danger to us? And even if it *is* a danger to us, how can you decide so swiftly to destroy such a unique life-form, without exploring other options first?"

"If Wanderer is so compassionate about humanoids," the captain countered, "then ask it why it didn't inform us at once that Hoshi was ill? I had to send someone from sickbay down to her lab to find her. She was unconscious."

"Perhaps . . ." T'Pol began, then fell silent. At last she admitted, "Wanderer was capable of notifying me, if not those in sickbay. I cannot explain this. Perhaps it was a cultural misunderstanding. Perhaps Wanderer misinterpreted what happened and thought she was dead or asleep, or that there was no point in informing us, since there was nothing we could do for her."

The captain let go an audible, frustrated breath. "Look, I know I have nothing more than a hunch. But it *is* a reasonable one. We've got to find out whether Wanderer is responsible for all the deaths, and how we can protect our people."

"Well, it doesn't like engineering," Trip said. "So a lot of people can camp out here. But I don't think we can fit sixty unless we stack 'em like dinner plates."

"The warp engines bother it," Archer said. "We've got to figure out why, so you can rig something that'll protect everyone—maybe even drive it from the vessel."

Trip managed to make a snicker sound grim. "Right. I'll just build another mini-warp engine with the spare parts lying around here."

"If it comes to that," Archer said, in a tone that conveyed he wasn't joking. He stepped over to a bulkhead and found the nearest companel. "Archer to sickbay."

"Cutler here." She sounded on the verge of collapse herself.

Don't you ever sleep, Ensign? he almost asked, but there was no time. Instead he told her, "I need you to bring all the patients in sickbay to engineering. Bring beds, life-support, whatever they need . . . but I want you and them to stay up here for a while."

"Excuse me, sir?"

"I'll explain everything in time. It's something of an emergency. Get as many hands as you need to help out. Archer out." He turned to Trip and T'Pol.

"Aren't you a bit ahead of yourself, Captain?" the Vulcan asked. "We don't even know that Wanderer is dangerous."

"That's what you and I are going to find out now," Archer said. "I'll need you to help me communicate with it. But first, we're going to stop by the armory."

Trip glanced at him. "You really think a phase pistol's gonna stop that thing if it gets mad?"

Archer shrugged. "You've got a better idea?"

Without moving a muscle in her face or deviating from her normal calm intonation even slightly, T'Pol managed to convey cool disdain for the notion. "Commander Tucker has a point, sir. Phase pistols are likely to be quite useless if in fact Wanderer is a danger to us. And there is no point in your accompanying me to speak to Wanderer, given that you do not feel safe. I am perfectly capable of asking it whatever questions you wish. I am quite certain it will not harm me."

Archer was by no means as certain—but he was willing to accept T'Pol's offer so that he could accomplish other things in the interim. "Very well, Sub-Commander. Although I want it noted that I'm gravely concerned for your safety, and am ordering you to arm yourself."

"And I must refuse, sir."

Archer could feel no anger: like Trip, he doubted whether a phase pistol would protect T'Pol if Wanderer decided to attack. He could only hope that, having communicated directly with T'Pol, Wanderer would have some compunctions about harming her.

T'Pol found Wanderer still lingering in the laboratory where Hoshi had been working. The creature was still hovering near the main computer databanks—it needed no terminal or viewer to access information, but apparently absorbed it directly from the computers themselves.

T'Pol crossed the threshhold, stood beside the creature, and remained silent—voice silent, thoughts silent, mind still, for she did not wish to communicate inadvertently any of her previous conversation with the captain. If Wanderer was innocent, she had no wish to offend; and if the creature was guilty, she did not wish to give it notice of the preparations to defend the crew, lest it retaliate.

For a full minute, Wanderer continued working on accessing the database. T'Pol waited patiently, but when her gaze fell on Hoshi's now abandoned station, she noticed something odd: a very slight scorching around the terminal data input area. She moved toward the area, and drew a fingertip over the darkened spot, then examined it.

Fine ash.

She pressed a control to eject the data disk— nothing emerged, and when she peered more carefully into the drive, she discovered a layer of black cinders. The disk had apparently been incinerated.

She turned to the energy creature—blue, roiling, and silent.

"Wanderer, do you know what happened to the Oani medical logs?"

Wanderer did not reply. Had T'Pol been capable of feeling surprise, she would have done so; the most obvious conclusion she could arrive at, given the apparently impossible, complete incineration of the Oani logs, was that Hoshi had discovered information that Wanderer had not wanted her to see.

Which led, inevitably, to the next, more unpleasant conclusion: that Wanderer had, in fact, been responsible for the destruction of the Oanis, and the weakness affecting the *Enterprise* crew members.

For herself, T'Pol felt no fear: instead, she felt a driving curiosity to know the full truth before she died. If Wanderer chose to kill her, the very fact of her death would serve the captain as notice that his theory was correct, so she would feel no sense of loss, no regret. Once more, she addressed the entity. "Ensign Sato became ill in this laboratory, while working. Yet you did not notify me of her illness. Is there some reason that you did not?"

Again, silence.

"It is interesting," T'Pol noted, "that the data logs we retrieved from the Oani people have been destroyed. Did you destroy them?"

When Wanderer again did not answer, T'Pol continued. "Your lack of response is perplexing." She paused. "I have postulated a theory—that you feed off the energy field created by humanoid bodies. Is this correct?"

At last, Wanderer spoke. *I do not feed off sentient humanoids.*

T'Pol was at once intrigued. "If you do not feed off humanoids, then how do you feed?"

Wanderer paused a time before communicating again. *I do not feed off* sentient *humanoids.*

A disturbing realization settled over T'Pol—rather like the sensation she had felt when she realized she had caused the *ch'kariya's* death.

"All living humanoids are, save for ancephalic clones, sentient."

That is not true. The humanoids you have chosen to travel with, for example, are nonsentient.

"Your contention is absurd. You need merely contact them mentally to see that they are sentient. The fact that I am able to communicate with them, and that they have been able to construct this starship, is proof enough."

They are not sentient.

"On what do you base this conclusion?"

I cannot communicate with them. Their minds are insufficiently sensitive to my efforts at contact. Therefore they are not sentient. You, however, are. Your mind is organized and sufficiently open to nonverbal contact.

"And therefore, you feel justified in killing them in order to maintain your own existence?"

According to your databanks, your people eat plant matter. Do they consider themselves murderers of those plants?

"You cannot compare plants with human beings," T'Pol countered dryly. "Plants do not possess the form of consciousness we call self-awareness." She paused. "Speaking in terms of evolution, there are very few differences between Vulcans and humans."

I cannot contact humans.

"Regardless, the fact remains that they are sentient. They suffer when you feed off them. They grieve the loss of their peers. I assume that you were unable to contact the Oanis as well."

Wanderer kept silent.

"Then you have destroyed an entire world of peace-loving beings," T'Pol said. "You can hardly claim to be a pacifist yourself."

You hold primitive beliefs, because you are close to being primitive yourself. Your own similarities to the humans blind you to your differences from them.

"I submit that your belief system has blinded you to the damage you have caused."

Clearly, I cannot reason with you on this issue. And Wanderer disappeared abruptly—simply vanished, without apparent movement—from the spot.

T'Pol stared at the now empty space with a sense of failure. She had hoped, logically, to persuade the creature to find an alternative food source, since it claimed to value peace so highly. Yet how could she persuade it that humans—and Denobulans, for that matter—possessed true consciousness, when Wanderer could not sense the existence of their minds?

And now that the truth had been revealed, how could she prevent Wanderer from destroying the rest of the *Enterprise* crew at will?

In engineering, Cutler and a number of assistants had already brought down the three stricken victims—Phlox, Reed, and Hoshi—on portable beds, and set up a makeshift sickbay of

143

sorts. But there had been only one portable life-support, and Cutler had decided, with the professional steadiness worthy of the most senior chief medical officer, that Phlox, the weakest, would have access to it.

Amazingly, Hoshi and Reed continued breathing on their own—there had been some uncertainty as to whether their life functions would fail without the equipment available only in sickbay.

Cutler herself looked ragged, ready to fail at any moment, despite the fact that she was still distraught over the disappearance of the Oani corpse. None of the medics in sickbay had managed to locate it. The captain couldn't help wondering whether Wanderer was somehow responsible.

"That's it," Archer said, once the patients were set up. "You're off-duty, Ensign."

Tucker led her to an out-of-the-way corner of engineering, where she lay on the deck, hand tucked beneath her head, and fell fast asleep. Archer envied her.

But this was no time for him to rest; he went over to the nearest bulkhead companel and pressed the shipwide broadcast control. "This is the captain speaking . . ."

His utterance was interrupted by a decidedly shrill burst of static. He grimaced and made the beginnings of a gesture to cover his ears, but instead terminated the channel, then tried again.

"This is the capt—"

The speaker screeched, this time so loud Archer succeeded in clapping his hands over his ears. *"Dammit!"* He lowered one hand just long enough to punch the control, cutting off the sound.

It was enough to totally distract Trip, who had been sitting on his haunches in his engineer's trance, scanning the warp engine with a sensor newly calibrated to pick up the most sensitive energy fluctuations. He scowled over his shoulder at Archer. "What the heck is *that?*"

Archer had his suspicions, but did not answer; he gave it one more try, this time choosing a single channel. "Archer to bridge."

Another squeal. The captain punched a control and tried sickbay, only to grimace again at the annoying static. Admitting defeat, he cut off the channel for the final time. Communications were definitely out.

"Coincidence?" Trip asked dryly.

"Too much of one. Sounds like T'Pol has already had that interesting little talk with our friend." He did not add, *Let's hope she comes back;* he was utterly concerned she would not, and the thought that Wanderer, who had so deceived her, might now harm her filled him with outrage.

"Captain."

He glanced in the direction of the urgent summons to see one of Cutler's commandeered medical assistants—a lieutenant from the science department—waving frantically at him.

Beside the lieutenant, lying on the portable bed, Hoshi Sato was blinking and looking at her surroundings, her brow wrinkled with confusion.

Archer was next to her in a heartbeat, overwhelmed with delight at this unexpected turn. "Hoshi! How do you feel?"

"Gross," Hoshi croaked. "Am I delirious, or are we in engineering?"

Archer grinned. "You're not delirious."

She paused, and then a look of horrified remembrance came over her features. "Oh my God—Wanderer! Captain—"

"We know," Archer said gently. "Wanderer killed the Oanis. Wanderer apparently tried to kill you. That's why we're in engineering—apparently, the warp drive emits some form of energy that disrupts it. We're hoping that'll keep us safe from it. Given the fact that I'm talking to you, I'm going to say that's a pretty sound assumption."

"No, you don't understand!" Hoshi was so agitated, she clasped the captain's wrist. "Kano—the Oani woman, the corpse that we brought up from the planet's surface. Wanderer used it—animated it. I guess it needed a humanoid in order to interface with the computer."

Archer felt himself pale. "My God . . . Ensign Cutler said a corpse was missing from sickbay."

Hoshi's expression remained distraught. "Captain, Wanderer is using it."

For an instant, Archer closed his eyes and shook his head. After a long silence passed between them both, the captain said at last, "All right. At least we know what we're up against. But we'll find a way to put a stop to it."

They both looked up at the sound of the doors to engineering opening. T'Pol entered—all in one piece—and despite the recent horrifying revelation, Archer couldn't hold back a faint grin.

"T'Pol! Thank God you're all right!"

The door closed behind the Vulcan; she paused just beyond it, and studied Archer with ostensible detachment. "No deity was involved, Captain. The fact is that Wanderer considers me 'sentient,' and therefore will not harm me."

She said it with utter coolness—but Archer felt he detected a hint of humor in her pretense at literalness.

Trip, however, took umbrage. His work trance broken, he turned his head—body still crouching—to address T'Pol. "You're saying that Wanderer considers us something less?"

She remained unruffled. "Correct. Because it could not communicate with you humans—or with the Oanis—it feels it has the right to feed off your bodies' electrical impulses."

"Let me guess," Trip said sarcastically. "It's a

personal friend of Ambassador Soval's." He turned back to his work.

"You are free to insult my superior," T'Pol said, "but you might find it consoling to know that Wanderer considers us Vulcans 'primitive,' and just barely sentient. It therefore ignored my attempts to reason with it."

"I think it killed the Oanis," Hoshi said weakly, "by convincing another alien, a Shikedan, that the Oanis were dying from a microbe."

T'Pol's upswept brows lifted slightly at the sight of the now-conscious ensign. "Ensign Sato," she said. "I assume Wanderer attacked you when you learned something . . . inconvenient."

Hoshi nodded. "It was so sad . . . The Oanis were so peace-loving that they wouldn't kill even a microbe. They accepted what Wanderer said without question, and died without investigating the cause of their deaths any further." She shook her head. "Can you imagine . . . being willing to die rather than kill a virus? To let your whole civilization die?"

T'Pol considered this in silence.

"Even more horrible . . . Wanderer is using the body of the female Oani we brought aboard. She—it—the corpse appeared in the lab before I collapsed, and was entering commands into the main computer."

T'Pol was again silent a time; then she asked,

quite bluntly, "Are you sure it was not a hallucination, Ensign?"

Hoshi scowled. "Of course I'm sure!"

"All right," Archer interrupted. "I don't mean to cut you off, Hoshi. The story of the Oanis is a tragic one, and I mean to see that we don't repeat it ourselves. Here's the situation: Since Wanderer doesn't like engineering, I want to get as many of our people down here as we can before it decides to feed again. The problem is, communications systems are down. I can't raise anyone on this ship. I assume Wanderer has figured things out and is causing the problem."

"I'm feeling better," Hoshi said, unconvincingly. She struggled into a sitting position. "I can try to see if there's a way around the communications problem. . . ."

"Lie back down," Archer snapped, with such vehemence that she complied at once. "So T'Pol, if it's true that Wanderer won't harm you, I want you to go alert everyone aboard the ship." He paused. "Frankly, I'm concerned. If Wanderer knows that *we* know it's a killer, there's nothing to keep it from suddenly attacking everyone."

"I would not be so certain of that," T'Pol said. "It could easily have attacked everyone when it came on board, without our being aware of it. But Lieutenant Reed and Doctor Phlox and Ensign Sato all collapsed at different times."

"And the medical logs indicated the Oanis

didn't all die at once, either," Hoshi chimed in. "Maybe it's not *capable* of attacking more than one person at a time."

Several yards away, Trip Tucker at last rose from his crouching position beside the warp engine and looked up from his scanner at the captain. "Like I said: Maybe it's full. Maybe it can only digest so much at one sitting."

"I think you're on to something," Archer said. "I also think T'Pol and I need to get going: someone's got to warn the rest of the crew, and get them headed this way—the sooner, the better."

"They can't all fit in here, Captain," Tucker advised him.

"I know," Archer said. "But we can protect at least half of them, maybe more." He turned to the Vulcan. "Let's go."

Eight

FIFTEEN MINUTES before the morning shift was to begin, Ensign Travis Mayweather stepped from the turbolift onto the *Enterprise* bridge . . . and got an unsettling surprise.

Mayweather always reported for duty fifteen minutes early . . . and he had never, ever arrived on the bridge without seeing Captain Archer already seated in his command chair, and Sub-Commander T'Pol standing nearby at the science station.

Today, the captain's chair stood empty, and the science station was deserted. In fact, the bridge was empty save for a skeleton crew: Ensign Katerina Borovsky at the helm, and Ensign Ahmed al Saed at communications. No one stood at tactical to replace the fallen Lieutenant Reed.

"Mayweather!" Borovsky said, pronouncing the *w* almost, but not quite like, a *v.* Her expression went from anxious to relieved—clearly, she was glad to see a familiar face. She was auburn-haired, with what Mayweather considered traditionally Russian coloring—light brown eyes, and pale skin with a pinkish cast, that flushed easily. It flushed now, at the sight of Mayweather, who knew he was considered an old salt among the less space-traveled crew.

"Where's the captain?" Mayweather asked, with a nod at the empty chair.

"Lieutenant Meir was supposed to fill in at command." This time al Saed spoke. He was in his thirties, older than Mayweather and Borovsky, a bit shy and sweet-natured. Dark-skinned and athletic, he nursed what he thought was a secret crush on Borovsky, but which was public knowledge to the entire crew, including Borovsky. "She never reported."

"Ahmed tried to raise her," Borovsky added, with her typical "take charge" attitude. "He got a channel but no answer. So he contacted sickbay— same thing. No one answering. As a last resort, he tried the captain's quarters. . . ."

"Let me guess," Mayweather said.

Borovsky nodded. "No dice. And now there's this horrible static on all channels." She finally paused, disappointment clear in her expression and tone. "We were hoping you'd know whether the captain was all right. We heard earlier about Hoshi. . . ."

"Hoshi?" Mayweather stiffened, alarmed.

"She collapsed," Borovsky said sadly. "I'm so sorry. I'm not thinking straight. Of course you wouldn't know. . . ." She and Hoshi were good friends; Hoshi always teased Borovsky by mimicking her Russian accent perfectly, which only made Borovsky laugh and slap Hoshi on the back with such force the exolinguist would feign a coughing fit after. Mayweather had socialized with the two of them a bit, and knew better than to try to bluff at poker when either Borovsky or Hoshi was playing.

Mayweather had known that Reed had collapsed—he had voluntarily been among the last to receive his immunization against radiation sickness; but now, to hear about Hoshi . . . The sight of the empty bridge took on a sudden ominousness, and he could understand why Borovsky and al Saed were so desperate for news of the captain. Without communications, it was easy to imagine the worst.

And right now, Mayweather was imagining the worst himself. "Go ahead, you two," he told the other officers. "I'll take it from here. Someone else is bound to show up."

"I won't leave," Al Saed said, his polite, gentle voice managing to convey an unshakable firmness. "Not until the captain orders me."

"I could order you," Mayweather said. "No point in stressing your immune system. And if communications aren't working—"

"If communications aren't working, I have to do my best to repair them." Al Saed frowned. "Although I've never come across anything like this in simulations."

"Gremlins," said Mayweather. "Welcome to space."

"Besides, you can't order me," al Saed pointed out. "We share the same rank."

"Well, I've been in space longer." Mayweather figured he could make noises about being part of the senior bridge crew, but it seemed pointless, especially if communications had suffered critical damage.

Al Saed smiled mildly, thin lips and broad black brows curving into mirror-image crescents. "I'm afraid that doesn't count."

"Suit yourself." Mayweather shrugged. He went over to the helm and motioned for Borovsky to move out of his seat. "Go on. You're definitely off duty, Ensign."

"I'll wait at tactical," said Borovsky, as she slid out and stood. "At least until we figure out what's going on."

Mayweather opened his mouth to protest, then closed it. He understood. While the bridge was always emptier, quieter during the evening shift, this morning it was disturbingly empty and quiet.

Something was amiss—they all knew it—and he realized that, were he in Borovsky's situation, nothing could have forced him to leave. He simply nodded as he settled into his station . . . then almost bolted to his feet again as a shrill blast of static assaulted his ears.

"*Good* lord . . ."

"Sorry," al Saed said sheepishly. "I keep having to reduce the volume when I test the different channels. It just keeps getting louder. . . ." He sighed. "I just can't find anything wrong with the equipment itself. If only Hoshi . . ." He did not finish the statement.

Mayweather tried not to finish it silently for him. Instead, the helmsmen focused on the readings before him: Engines humming along at a dizzying warp four. Course set for heading seven-zero-four-zero, which should lead to the planet called Shikeda, where they should be able to resolve the dispute about whether the disease afflicting the crew was caused by radiation or a microbe.

Which of course led Mayweather to the thought that perhaps *he* should have gone down in Hoshi's place—although that wouldn't have made sense. Or perhaps he should have gone down in the captain's place; why should the commander of the starship, the most vital member of the crew, be the one to take all the risks? Or he could have replaced Reed. Dr. Phlox, of course—well, they had needed a doctor because it was a medical emergency. But it still didn't seem fair. . . .

Al Saed's companel let out another shrill blast.

"My *God*," Mayweather said, but this time he wasn't reacting to the noise; he half rose from his station, was knocked back down to a sitting position by the helm console itself, and remained there, gaping at the readout in front of him.

As he watched, the course heading began slowly to change, from seven-zero-four-zero to six-nine-five-two, to five-seven-five-zero, to four-eight-five-nine. . . .

Mayweather began slamming controls. None had any effect on the course heading; in response, he tried to revert to manual, and began pressing controls even more frantically.

Borovsky moved beside him to stare down at the impossible sight. "What is it?"

"Our course is changing," Mayweather gasped. "We're turning around. . . ." He batted at a few more switches, reverted from manual to computer and back. Nothing worked. "Helm is unresponsive."

"That can't be," Borovsky said, yet as she watched Mayweather follow the book on every possible procedure, she was at a loss to come up with a suggestion. She peered down with him, watching as the heading continued to change: three-two-seven-four, two-nine-nine-eight . . .

Even al Saed left his repair attempt at communications to come over to the helm and stare with them.

"This is crazy!" Borovsky exclaimed in frustration. "What could cause this?"

"Nothing," Mayweather said. Nothing except someone intentionally adjusting the course heading by overriding the helm controls—and why would anyone aboard *Enterprise* do that?

As he spoke, the bridge doors opened behind them; the trio turned.

"Captain Archer!"

All three officers called out his name almost simultaneously; Mayweather's grin was huge. "Sir, we were so worried something had—"

"There's no time to explain right now," Archer said. "We're in great danger from Wanderer. The only safe place on this ship is engineering; I need you three to head there right now." When they hesitated, the captain added, "That's an order!"

"Sir." Mayweather remained at his post, and gestured down at the aberrant console readings. "I'd leave, but the helm is malfunctioning wildly. We're off course by almost . . ." He glanced down swiftly. "One-eighty degrees, sir."

Archer wasted no time; he literally ran to the console and looked down—just as the course heading adjusted to zero-zero-zero-zero, then stayed there.

"Earth," Mayweather said at last, his tone hushed. "We're headed back to Earth."

"Wanderer," Archer said, with a darkness in his tone the ensign did not understand. "Leave it, Ensign. The three of you report down to engineering. Stay in there until I advise you otherwise. *Now!*"

Mayweather had no choice but to comply, leaving behind him on the bridge viewscreen a dizzying sweep of stars.

"Lieutenant Meir?" Archer called.

He'd been going through the senior and junior officers' cabins, routing people to engineering, while T'Pol had agreed to take the noncom personnel, as well as the science department and kitchen. One of the officers had agreed to stop by the captain's quarters and pick up Porthos. So far, everything had been going a little faster than Archer had hoped—although he had been infuriated by the realization that Wanderer now had control of the helm, and was sending *Enterprise* back to Earth.

We're not the Oanis, Archer told himself firmly. *We're not like any other humanoids Wanderer has encountered—we're going to fight back, and we're going to win.*

Those officers who were off-duty had answered their buzzers almost at once, even those who had supposedly been sleeping—the situation with

Wanderer had left everyone on edge, more vigilant than usual. But Meir wasn't answering—and the fact that Mayweather had mentioned that she hadn't reported for duty gave Archer the boldness to override the lock on the door without a second thought.

As he had feared, Meir was inside—lying neatly on her bunk, hands folded primly on her chest, long blond hair no longer bound in its usual chignon but spread around her, as if she were a sleeping princess from a fairy tale. Archer went to her at once and bent down to scoop her up into his arms. Once she was in engineering, he hoped, she'd be protected from Wanderer and might even regain consciousness as Hoshi had. . . .

But after he slid his arms beneath her shoulders and under the crook of her knees and began to lift her, he paused and studied her more closely. Her head lolled to one side; her features were slack. She looked to be unconscious, but some atavistic instinct told Archer something was wrong. With his free hand, he reached for her neck, and laid his first two fingers where her carotid artery should be.

The flesh there was slightly—only slightly—cool.

Archer could feel no pulse. He lifted his fingers and tried again, in a different spot, then another one, then another.

Lieutenant Meir's heart was no longer beating.

Archer let her go and for an instant—no more—permitted himself to sink the rest of the way to the deck. He gritted his teeth and growled.

"Bastard! You *bastard!*"

And he thought of the dead man in the Oani hospital, his features contorted with rage.

How could this have happened? None of the other stricken had died. He remembered Trip saying, *Maybe it's still full.*

Then he thought of Hoshi coming to; and realized that it no longer had her, or Phlox, or Reed to feed on.

"Bastard," he whispered, and pushed himself to his feet. He ran on; there were others to warn, to get to engineering. But before he left, he promised Meir silently that he would return.

A woman's voice, muffled but familiar: *He seems to have stabilized, Commander. I think he's coming to. . . .*

Malcolm Reed opened his eyes, feeling very much as he had the morning after he'd nicked a bottle of gin from his parents' liquor cabinet and awakened with his first hangover.

Leering over him was the face of Commander Trip Tucker.

Reed groaned. "I knew it," he muttered, and put a hand to his forehead. "I've died and gone to hell."

"No such luck, you little devil," Tucker drawled, in the Southern accent that evoked the image in Reed's head of vowels and consonants slithering down a slide coated in oil. Tucker was grinning broadly, apparently enormously pleased. It took Reed some time, in his weakened state, to realize that Tucker was actually pleased to see *him*. "I'm afraid you get to stick around with us a little while longer. And that land in Argentina is still safe and in the family name."

"I was . . ." Reed sat up and rubbed his forehead vigorously, as if trying to stimulate his memory. "I was in sickbay. Giving injections. Did I pass out?"

Smiling, Hoshi was standing beside Tucker with Porthos in her arms. "You did. Just like Doctor Phlox—his vital signs are improving, he should be back with us pretty soon. And just like I did. But we're okay now."

Reed finally found the strength to smile back. "So . . . it wasn't radiation poisoning then, was it? A sickness, then, and you've found the cure?"

"Neither," Trip said, and he and Hoshi shared a dismal, if knowing, glance. "It was Wanderer."

Reed drew back. "I *knew* it!"

"It'd have been nice if you'd known it a little sooner," Trip said. He opened his mouth to say more, but Reed was becoming more aware of his surroundings.

"Good lord," he interrupted. "What am I doing in *engineering?*" He looked around him, for the first time taking everything in. Phlox indeed rested only a matter of feet away, still unconscious on a cot, with a portable life-support system propped against the nearby bulkhead. Most perplexingly, though, several officers from different departments were milling about, some seated, others standing, all talking in low tones and seeming restless, as if they didn't know quite what to do with themselves. The door kept opening and closing as more people entered.

"Seems that Wanderer doesn't like engineering," Hoshi offered.

Trip nodded. "That's something I'd like to talk to you about. Right now, the only protection we've got against that creature is staying in here. . . . We need to figure out exactly why Wanderer won't come near here, find a way to amplify it, direct it—"

"—And use it to blow the thing to bits," Reed finished for him. He rubbed his aching head again. "Let me be the first to volunteer." He swung his legs over the edge of the bed and put his feet on the floor, gingerly.

"Easy." Trip gripped Reed's elbow and steadied him as he stood. Reed grimaced; the metal deck was cold against his bare feet.

"Does anyone have my boots?"

The medic standing over Phlox glanced up.

"I'm afraid we left them in sickbay, Lieutenant."

Reed scowled; as he did, T'Pol stepped up beside him, so quietly and quickly that he recoiled and almost lost his balance.

"Forgive me, Lieutenant," she said, with that flat, neutral tone. "I did not mean to startle you." She turned at once to Trip. "Commander Tucker, as you can see from the growing crowd here, we are soon to be faced with a dilemma. I have notified the personnel assigned me to report to engineering, and I assume the captain has almost finished notifying his group."

"I see what you mean," Trip said. Ever since Reed had come to, the stream of people entering engineering had been constant; if it continued much longer, there would no longer be standing room available.

"Once the room is filled to capacity, perhaps we should ask volunteers to remain outside. Certainly, I can remain outside safely. However, essential personnel—such as you and Mr. Reed, the captain, and Doctor Phlox—should remain inside."

She looked pointedly at the beagle in Hoshi's arms.

"Oh no you don't—sir," Hoshi said. "I'll go outside before I let you put Porthos outside."

Reed sighed. "Ah, to be a dog in these civilized times."

"I can tell you exactly what'll happen," Trip told

163

the Vulcan. "Ask for volunteers, and *everyone*'ll volunteer."

T'Pol managed to convey skepticism with a simple millimeters-high lift of her eyebrows.

"We'll draw straws," Trip said.

"But that is entirely arbitrary."

"Precisely, Sub-Commander." Trip looked toward the doorway, and his brow furrowed a bit. "Or we could wait for the captain to make a decision when he gets here. I wonder what's keeping him. . . ."

At that moment, Archer had discovered the last unwarned crew member, a young male ensign, unconscious on his cabin deck. A quick medical check revealed slowed respiration and pulse. Wanderer had been feeding again, and that realization, along with anger over the death of Lieutenant Meir, filled Archer with uncommon energy despite his lack of sleep. With surprisingly little effort, he bent down on one knee, slung the unconscious ensign over his shoulder, then pushed himself to his feet.

"I won't let you have this one," Archer said, to an enemy that was no longer there.

He staggered through the doorway into the gray metal corridor. In the simulated daylight, it was now hearteningly empty; the crew had taken their captain's warning seriously. Archer could only hope that all of them made it safely to engineering, and that T'Pol had had success with her mission.

He could not help wondering whether his discovery of the unconscious ensign meant that someone else had recovered—Reed or Phlox—which had forced Wanderer to feed again.

Archer gasped beneath the weight of the unconscious crewman; he wanted to run down the corridor, realizing that Wanderer might need to strike again, but he could manage no better than a slow jog. And as soon as he got the ensign to engineering, he intended to go back for Meir's body unless he was needed to perform a duty critical to destroying Wanderer. It had seemed wrong to leave her in her bunk; he at least wanted to see her body properly stored in sickbay, so that it could be returned to relatives or given proper space burial.

Archer made it down the corridor toward the turbolift, with the thought of heading up to engineering. . . .

But as he neared the lift doors, their color changed from off-white to blue-green. The air in front of them began to swirl and ripple, like the crashing of waves in a turbulent sea. . . .

"Wanderer," Archer said aloud, his tone flinty with hate. "Get out of my way."

It was a futile command, of course; the creature remained, shimmering, growing larger until it blocked the entire corridor. Archer was left with no way to advance, only retreat.

But anger and determination would not permit him to do so. Gently, he knelt on one knee, then carefully lowered the ensign to the deck.

It was time to discover exactly how truthful Wanderer had been. No one, after all, had touched the creature in order to know what the effect would be. And all of Wanderer's attacks had apparently occurred without direct contact with its victim. Wanderer had been careful to request right away that no one touch it.

Was it possible that it had to be careful to absorb only so much energy at one time? What would happen if it accidentally was exposed to too much?

Archer rose, drew a deep breath, then rushed the creature.

The instant he entered Wanderer was palpable: The ship around him dissolved, and the world turned blue-green, dazzling, electric. The hair on Archer's head and body stood straight upright; the skin on his forearms, his back, and the backs of his legs turned to gooseflesh. And then he was blinded—not by darkness, but by light, white brilliance, that shot up from the base of his spine straight up through the top of his skull. He felt caught up by a current—a current of electricity, a current of water, of oceans and tides, that pulled him along and spun him, round and round till he cried out and lost all sense of himself. . . .

A clap of thunder. Archer was heaved to the deck, hard, his skull connecting with metal so swift and fast that the pain was no more than a flash, bright and hot, before the darkness came.

Nine

CHARLES "TRIP" TUCKER had a natural tendency to be good-humored, even during crises, or times when he didn't get much sleep; but the way things were going at the moment, every shred of Tucker's good nature had long ago vanished. They were stacked like sardines in engineering, and the radiant body heat was making Trip start to sweat; apparently, the environmental computer had failed to compensate for the crowding. A handful of crew members sat outside the closed door in the corridor, waiting their turn to come stand inside the safety of engineering. Given T'Pol's determination (and obvious lack of concern for the human concept of personal space), she'd managed to get more people than Trip had thought possible into engineering. He had to give her credit; but at the same time, he longed for some room to stretch out so he could think.

It didn't help matters that the dozens of people surrounding him were all talking to ward off the boredom and anxiety; snippets of conversation drifted down from the overhead deck, as well, where uniformed personnel were practically hanging off the railings. Trip was used to quiet, and the hum of his engines, and all these people in such a small amount of space were starting to drive him crazy. Dr. Phlox was conscious and alert now, on his feet, and speculating about the nature of Wanderer and its effect on Denobulans and humans with an enthusiasm that grated.

Mayweather, standing rather than sitting at the nearest computer console because there simply wasn't room, turned to T'Pol beside him. The two were a mere arm's stretch from Tucker and Reed, so it was impossible for Trip to ignore the conversation.

"It just isn't responding, Sub-Commander. We're still headed for Earth, no matter what overrides I try. . . ."

"Same here," Hoshi chimed in from a nearby companel. "All communications frequencies are jammed."

Until Archer returned, T'Pol was in charge, monitoring the ship's condition and seeing to it that officers in engineering regularly traded places with those sitting out in the corridor.

"Keep trying," T'Pol ordered them both.

As she did, Malcolm Reed looked glumly down at the handheld scanner in his grasp, then back up at Tucker. "Energy fluctuations and fairy dust—that's what Wanderer's made of. It doesn't make sense that engineering would bother it. The engines are sealed tightly enough so they don't irradiate *us*—why they should bother something *made* of radiation . . ." He clicked his tongue.

"Quit stating the obvious," Trip snapped, with such force that Reed drew back in mild surprise, eyebrows lifted.

"It's not my fault, Commander."

"I know," Trip growled. "It's just that there's got to be something more to Wanderer than our systems are capable of detecting."

T'Pol had overheard the exchange—why shouldn't she, with those ears? Trip thought—and turned toward the two men. "I assure you, I accurately recalled the entire range of readings our scanners detected when we first encountered Wanderer."

The computers—and that information—were of course unavailable now, given the fact that Wanderer had figured out enough about the ship to render the computers, helm, and communications inaccessible. *Thank goodness it doesn't like the warp drive, or we'd be dead in the water. . . .* But T'Pol had listed in detail what the sensors had picked up on Wanderer's physical composition:

various types of radiation, mostly harmless, others from which Wanderer was actually shielding *Enterprise;* and different types of energy fluxes, most notably electromagnetic pulses.

"I believe you, Sub-Commander," Trip replied, very seriously. "But I have a suggestion."

The Vulcan dropped her chin and waited expectantly.

"We're trying to create a new device that will disrupt Wanderer's physical form. My question is: Why reinvent the wheel? Why not get a good old-fashioned phase pistol, set it on kill, and take a shot at the creature?" He did not suggest a stun blast, since that was designed to emit a frequency that induced unconsciousness in humanoids. Logically, it would probably do nothing at all to the entity.

"No," T'Pol replied, with finality.

Trip persisted. "Why not?"

"A phase pistol is designed to disrupt living cells. I fail to see how it would affect radiation."

"But it might displace an electromagnetic pulse—which might disrupt Wanderer enough to cause a problem. At least slow it down, if it doesn't kill it. It's worth a try."

"No, Commander. I thought I made it quite clear that you and Lieutenant Reed were to design a device that would protect us against Wanderer, not destroy it."

"Look, I'm not asking you to hurt it. I'm volunteering to go do the dirty work. We both know a phased blast probably won't be enough to kill the thing. Besides—the captain hasn't come back yet. You and I both know he's been gone too long. Someone is going to have to go look for him."

"The issue of the captain is a separate one," T'Pol said. "I am the logical choice to look for him, since Wanderer will not harm me. And I believe that there is a more peaceable solution than attempting to kill Wanderer with a phased blast." She paused. "Continue your work with Lieutenant Reed, Commander. I will go and find the captain." And without further comment, she exited engineering.

Trip and Reed watched her go.

"A brave woman," Reed said admiringly.

"Ah," Trip countered scornfully, "the thing's got a crush on her because she's more 'intelligent' than we are. It won't hurt her." He only wished, of course, that he could be as certain of that as he sounded. He looked sourly down at the scanner in Reed's hands. "So what do we try scanning for next? The engines don't emit any radiation to speak of, or vibration, or—"

"Pardon me," Doctor Phlox said jovially—too jovially, Trip felt, for the situation, which the Denobulan seemed to regard as more of an adventure than a life-threatening event. "I've been speculating on how Wanderer feeds . . ."

"So I've heard."

". . . and I have a theory: electricity."

"Electricity?" Trip blinked at the unexpected. Electricity seemed so primitive, so basic . . . and his engines certainly weren't emitting enough electricity to startle a mouse, much less something as vast and powerful as Wanderer.

"Well, as you know, all living things—well, most living things, especially humanoids—emit an electromagnetic charge. Subtle, very subtle . . . almost undetectable. But I've been thinking about some of the readings that I found on the Oanis, and there was a slight disturbance in their electrolytes. That could be caused by a number of things, but it would definitely affect their electrical system, if you will."

"Electrical system," Trip repeated. This was news to him; he hadn't gone beyond first year zoology in college, and had managed to avoid anatomy altogether because of his engineering major. Phlox's claim sounded pretty ridiculous.

"For example, the heartbeat," Phlox said. "Its rhythm is regulated by chemicals in the body that produce an electrical effect. In past centuries, humans actually used electricity to restore a heartbeat, or to correct an arrhythmic pulse."

"Really?" Reed was fascinated. "But certainly humans don't emit much electricity—"

"Hardly at all," Phlox said. "It's very faint; our medical scanners would have to be recalibrated to the utmost sensitivity in order to detect it. But it *is* there. And since Wanderer, according to what I've overheard from your and Commander Tucker's discussion, is partially composed of electromagnetic pulses, I couldn't help wondering whether there was a connection."

"So Wanderer feeds off the electromagnetic field generated by humanoid bodies . . ." Trip mused, thinking.

"It's just a possibility," Phlox said. "I could be completely wrong."

Trip didn't answer him; instead, he reached out for the scanner in Reed's hands. "Let me see that a minute." He fiddled with the controls, head down, then checked a reading. "Okay. I'm picking up a very faint electromagnetic field."

"It could be us," Reed offered. "Or all these people standing around."

"Hold on," Trip said. He shouldered his way past a few people until he stood directly next to the engines.

The reading rose very slightly. Trip's mood began to lighten.

"Anything?" Reed's tone was eager.

"Maybe," Trip said, his intonation rising on the last syllable. "Let's try a little experiment." He elbowed his way through the crowd until he found the doors to engineering; drawing in an anticipatory breath, he stepped through them.

On the other side of the doors, officers, seated on the deck, leaning against the bulkheads, lined the corridor. They looked up eagerly as Trip moved past.

"Time to swap?" one of them asked.

"Nope," Trip murmured, his gaze fixed on the readout. "Just a little experiment." And as the electromagnetic levels began to fall significantly the further he moved from engineering, the wider his smile became.

He wheeled about on one heel and went back, still grinning, into engineering.

Phlox and Reed were waiting for him, their expressions expectant, hopeful.

"We may just be on to something here," Trip said.

Captain.

Captain Archer, can you hear me?

Archer woke facedown, one cheek pressed to the unyielding, cold metal deck. His entire body, including his head, ached tremendously as though it had been slammed against the bulkhead repeatedly—at which point, he remembered his encounter with Wanderer and realized that he might very well *have* been slammed against a bulkhead.

He tried to roll to one side . . . and yelled aloud at the searing agony in his left shoulder, which felt as though it had been pulled from its socket.

"Captain." T'Pol's ever-steady, soothing tone penetrated Archer's pain and disorientation. He

175

lay motionless on his side, unwilling to move lest it aggravate his shoulder, and gazed sidewise up at the Vulcan, who crouched over him, her expression reassuringly neutral. "Allow me to assist you in rising. Your shoulder appears to be dislocated."

"Fine," Archer gasped. "I'm not going anywhere without help." He held perfectly still as the Vulcan leaned over him—so close that he felt the more-than-human warmth emanating from her body, and smelled a subtle fragrance similar to evergreen and citrus. Slender but surprisingly strong arms slipped around his body, enveloping him, and lifted him, swiftly but cautiously, to his feet. Even so, there was pain; Archer gritted his teeth, and let go a small yelp as he finally found his balance and stood on his own.

T'Pol stepped back and observed him critically, staring intently into his eyes. "Sir, I believe you may have a subdural hematoma."

"A what?" Archer asked groggily.

"I believe the vernacular is 'a concussion.' "

"I can believe it." Archer looked down at himself and took a quick assessment. The skin on his palms felt burned, even blistered, and a quick glance showed that the skin there was in fact reddened. . . . Even his face, arms, and back tingled, as if they, too, had been burned.

"I had a little encounter with Wanderer." He ran a hand cautiously over his hair; it felt as though it'd been standing on end, from static electricity. "I actually touched it—and I feel as though I've been struck by lightning."

"Wanderer has not left, sir. In fact, it was guarding you when I came off the turbolift . . . and from all indications, it does not intend to allow us access to it."

Archer followed her gaze: sure enough, blocking the way to the turbolift, Wanderer still hovered. But something about the creature had changed: it had deepened in color, becoming an intense sapphire, and its energy patterns were moving more swiftly than ever before; its shape was decidedly irregular.

"You didn't like that any more than I did, did you?" Archer asked it. The fact made little sense; Archer had half expected it to kill him—with the hope that it would win the ensign his life.

"It *has* changed in appearance," T'Pol confirmed.

Behind him, the unconscious ensign still lay where the captain had placed him. Holding his one useless arm to his side, Archer moved slowly toward the younger man; T'Pol hurried toward the ensign, crouched down, and felt his neck for a pulse. "Pulse is slow," she reported, "but steady."

Archer let go a grateful sigh, then looked up at their nemesis.

T'Pol seemed to read his thoughts. Rising, she said, "It will do no good to rush the creature again, sir—you will only injure yourself further. Perhaps I can reason with it."

"Be my guest," Archer said, without hiding his skepticism.

T'Pol approached the creature and said aloud, "Wanderer. Please move aside so that the captain and I can take the injured ensign to engineering."

The entity's brightness faded a bit; after a pause, T'Pol turned to the captain. "It refuses, sir. It says that it has a right to protect its own survival."

"To feed off us, you mean." Archer's lips twisted. "It's getting worried about lunch now that everyone's been moved to engineering."

T'Pol hesitated. "I don't believe it would intentionally harm me, Captain. I would like to try heading for the turbolift carrying the two of you—"

Wanderer obviously "said" something to her, for she broke off and turned toward the creature as if listening. After a pause, she told Archer dryly: "Apparently, Wanderer would not intentionally harm me—but it would not stop me from harming myself, and the two of you humans, if I chose to touch it. It warns that it will not move and allow us access to the turbolift."

"Well, if it won't move, then we'll just have to find a way around it. If we can't go up the turbolift, maybe we can try another way. . . ."

T'Pol nodded. She bent down and lifted the ensign in her arms, then followed the captain down the corridor toward the nearest access tunnel— but Wanderer moved into position in front of them, once again stopping them in their tracks.

"All right," Archer said. "Maybe we can't go up to engineering. But who's to say we can't go down?" He began to move in the opposite direction down the corridor, wincing with each step at the fresh knifelike pain in his arm and shoulder. He was headed for an access tunnel that led only one way: down to F-deck, which housed the torpedo bays and the armory.

T'Pol frowned. "What is your rationale for doing so?"

Archer knew the answer would draw resistance from his second-in-command, something he was in no mood for. Evasively, he replied, "Just consider it an order, Sub-Commander."

She said nothing further, merely followed him to the tunnel opening. She went first, easily slinging the unconscious ensign over one shoulder, then climbing down without effort.

For Archer, it was enormously awkward and precarious. He was forced to climb down one-handed—making him feel like he was a cadet undergoing obstacle training. At each rung, he had to let go and quickly grab for the next, leaving an instant where he was completely unstable. The disabled arm swung uselessly at his side; the stabs of pain emanated from the center of

Archer's spine through his shoulder and all the way down to his fingertips, causing him to gasp through gritted teeth.

Somehow, he made it down into the armory, where T'Pol waited, not even breathing heavily. Archer at once moved to the bulkhead where the phase rifles were stored and took one with his good hand.

T'Pol stood, silent and solemn.

"Don't worry, I'm not asking you to arm yourself," Archer said. He checked the setting on the rifle awkwardly, then hoisted the weapon to see if he could aim. It wasn't comfortable, but it would work.

"Captain," T'Pol says earnestly, "Wanderer is unlike any other life-form we have discovered. It may be the only one of its kind. To destroy it would be tantamount to committing the same crime it committed against the Oanis—genocide."

"Would you prefer it wiped out everyone on this ship, and on Earth, instead?"

"No. However, I am certain a third solution exists."

"Look, I don't want to kill it any more than you do. I doubt a blast from a phase rifle will do anything to it—I'm just hoping it'll disable the damned thing. But if it does kill it—well, I'm willing to take that chance." He moved from the armory toward the turbolift as T'Pol followed, the ensign still in her arms.

As he expected, Wanderer was waiting for them in front of the F-deck turbolift.

The sight of the creature evoked in Archer quite the opposite of compassion. He steadied the rifle against the right side of his body. "All right, Wanderer—you don't like the taste of me right now. How do you like the taste of this?"

He fired.

The brilliant beam bored through the air . . . and, as Archer had feared, directly through the energy creature, piercing the field of blue-green without effect, just as it would any spaceborne field of radiation or electromagnetic pulses.

The blast sailed through Wanderer so effortlessly, in fact, that it damaged the bulkhead behind the creature, searing through the metal and exposing the circuitry beneath.

Sparks flew. And a single electrical current—a blue-white surge of microlightning—crackled.

The current caught Wanderer's nebulous periphery. The creature writhed, pulsing forward suddenly in one direction like a reckless amoeba and turning an intense shade of cobalt so dazzling that Archer shielded his eyes from the glow.

"Captain," T'Pol said, "I believe we can attempt to board the turbolift."

The two of them hurried through the open doors while a distracted Wanderer continued to spasm and pulsate.

* * *

"Commander!" Hoshi shouted, over the din of an overcrowded engineering. "I've got an open channel!"

Trip Tucker looked up from the device he and Malcolm Reed had been working on. It was ridiculously simple, actually, so simple and old-fashioned that they'd had trouble finding parts for it—just a small electricity generator.

Hoshi's words gave Trip hope; he'd started to worry about the captain—and now, T'Pol. They'd been gone too long, and clearly had encountered Wanderer on their way . . . But the sudden reclamation of communications made Trip grin. His instincts told him Jonathan Archer was alive and well and giving Wanderer a run for its money.

"Contact Starfleet Command at once," he ordered cheerfully, rising from where he and Reed had been bent over their old-fashioned device. "Advise them of our situation."

"You've got it, sir."

The ride to D-deck, a mixture for Archer of agony and optimism, seemed to take longer than usual—an effect, no doubt, of the shooting pain in his shoulder and arm, and his eagerness to be back in the haven of engineering. Beside him, T'Pol stood silently, the ensign—several inches taller than she—cradled in her arms, while her posture remained straight and at ease, as if she were holding no more than an infant.

At last the turbolift stopped, and the doors opened onto D-deck, to Archer's relief; he had half expected Wanderer to recover and stall their journey before they reached the main engineering level. But now the engine room was only a corridor's stroll away. Archer moved swiftly out of the lift, clutching his affected arm to his side, gritting his teeth against the pain; T'Pol matched him stride for stride.

Yet before they made it even a third of the way to their destination, Archer stopped in his tracks at an unexpected sight—one that at first his concussion-fogged brain could not make sense of.

Lieutenant Meir, her blond hair in unkempt curls upon her shoulders, uniform disheveled, had just stepped into their path from an intersecting corridor; at the sight of them, she turned and faced them.

Archer was speechless. At first, he felt overwhelmed with joy: he had been wrong, Meir had been alive all along, simply unconscious, and had recovered. . . .

And then a darker realization overtook the joy. There was something deeply unnatural about the human woman's movements, something marionettelike.

Like any good sub-commander, T'Pol stepped into the breach at the captain's silence. "Lieutenant," she ordered. "Report at once to engineering."

Meir's eyes were open but sightless, directed at the other two officers, but unfocused. Her hand moved to her utility belt, and the phase pistol strapped there.

With his good hand, Archer seized T'Pol's shoulder and pushed her and her burden down just before Meir fired. At the same time, he dropped to the deck; the rush of adrenaline managed to make his shoulder's intolerable pain bearable.

"Meir's dead," he breathed to the downed Vulcan beside him. "Hoshi was right—she wasn't hallucinating. Wanderer has somehow reanimated the lieutenant."

The bright blast overhead streaked past them and seared open the bulkhead with the pervasive smell of scorched metal.

"The attack is not logical." T'Pol lay on her stomach, palms pressed to the deck beneath her collarbone; her normally perfect fringe of bangs was parted, and a stray brown wisp of hair stuck out above the rest. She turned her face toward the captain. "Her weapon is set to kill."

In the instant before Meir took inhumanly clumsy aim again, Archer saw that the Vulcan was right. It made no sense: if Wanderer wanted to keep Archer and the unconscious ensign from engineering so that it could feed off them, why not simply stun them?

Meir fired, jerkily, again, and Archer rolled. In the periphery of his vision, bedazzled by the phase-pistol blast, he saw T'Pol rise, leaving the ensign lying on the deck. The Vulcan charged the human woman, striking her at waist level and knocking her off her feet, onto her back. Her hand struck the metal deck with audible force; the phase pistol went skittering across the corridor.

T'Pol scrambled in the direction of the weapon. But Meir did not stay down long. Her body jerked to its feet as though yanked by an invisible wire attached to her sternum; she headed straight for the Vulcan.

At the same time, Archer struggled to his feet, clasping the injured arm against his side. He, too, made a dash for the weapon.

T'Pol reached it first. She seized the phase pistol and turned—at the same time, smoothly switching the setting from kill to stun.

"It doesn't matter!" Archer shouted. "She's already dead!"

But his words came too late. In the heartbeat it took T'Pol to turn and switch the weapon's setting, Meir charged.

T'Pol fired, the blast knocking the human's body backward.

How do you knock a corpse unconscious? Archer wondered. *How do you kill it?*

His question was answered immediately as Meir rose again, puppetlike, and headed once more for T'Pol. By this time, Archer was upon them both. With his good arm, he swung with all his strength at Meir, hoping at least to knock her off balance and allow T'Pol time to rise. The act of hitting another officer without restraint went against all of Archer's instincts, but he managed to strike the lieutenant with enough force to send her a staggering step sideways.

T'Pol leapt to her feet, phaser still in her hand.

"Set it on kill!" Archer commanded.

T'Pol hesitated.

And in that instant of hesitation, Meir struck Archer with a crushing blow to the midback—a blow stronger than any human, male or female, could have administered. He dropped to his knees, by sheer will refusing to go all the way down. "Shoot!" he cried hoarsely.

T'Pol fired.

Once again, the human woman went staggering back . . . then immediately returned and seized T'Pol's wrist. At the same time, Meir slammed the Vulcan's back against the wall, with such force that phase pistol dropped and T'Pol slid to the deck, dazed.

"No," Archer said, furious at himself, at his wounds, which left him unable to fight back. Wanderer would kill them now, and have his ship—yet even facing defeat, Archer could not permit himself to yield to it. He forced himself to his feet and drew a ragged breath, intending to hurl himself at Meir's body one last time. . . .

But Meir, apparently satisfied, picked up the

pistol and walked away down the corridor, intent on some other destination.

"What the . . . ?" Archer murmured, gasping, clutching his arm to his side. He staggered over to T'Pol, who sat, somewhat wide-eyed, against the bulkhead. "Are you okay?"

"I am . . . free of any significant injury." She glanced up at the captain. "Certainly, I am in better condition than you are."

"Thanks for noticing," Archer said wryly.

The Vulcan rose, apparently taken aback by Meir's sudden disappearance. "If Wanderer fears our informing the rest of the crew about its inability to tolerate electricity . . . why did it not kill us?"

"Obviously, it has a soft spot for Vulcans," Archer said. "But I don't understand why it didn't kill *me*." He paused. "It's planning something. The question is, what?"

Ten

IN ENGINEERING, Archer sat at one of the computer consoles while Dr. Phlox stood back (which, given the crowded conditions, was only a step or two) and studied the captain's left shoulder.

"T'Pol is correct on both counts, I would say," the doctor said genially. "You *do* have a dislocated shoulder—to use the vernacular—and you *do* have a concussion. We're fortunate on both counts. The concussion is very mild—a good thing, since I have no way of treating it without returning you to sickbay."

"How is the shoulder fortunate?" Archer groaned. Now that he, T'Pol, and the unconscious crewman were out of immediate danger, the pain in that quadrant of his body was reaching unbearable proportions.

Porthos, now back in Hoshi's arms, wriggled as close as possible to his master and licked Archer's face, covering it with spittle and warm dog breath. Not exactly medicine, but it would have to do.

Archer's faint smile came out a grimace. "Thanks, Porthos. Not now, buddy."

Phlox replied to Archer's question. "It's fortunate in that both Denobulans and humans are very similar in terms of skeletal structure. I actually can solve the problem of your shoulder with a simple physical manipulation. . . ." He leaned down over the captain, put one hand on the affected scapula and one hand on Archer's chest, and gave a swift, violent push.

Archer screamed.

Porthos snarled, teeth bared, and very nearly lunged out of Hoshi's arms at the doctor. Hoshi caught the beagle by the hind legs just in time and gathered him back into her arms, before he could take a piece out of Phlox's hands.

"I'm sorry, Porthos," Phlox told the dog. "But I dare say your master will be feeling much better now."

Archer sat straight, flexed the wounded shoulder—gingerly at first, then more firmly—and tested his arm by raising it. "It's true," he said, looking up at Phlox in amazement. "It's just a little tender. Thank you, Doctor. Now I have *another* reason to be glad you're back with us."

The Denobulan stood back and beamed. "Sometimes the best medicine is the simplest." He paused. "Sorry I can't help you with that headache yet. Or the slight burns on your skin."

"We've got better things to worry about right now," Archer said. Hoshi could no longer hold Porthos back; Archer took the dog from her, and let him burrow against the hollow of his chest.

Trip Tucker took a step forward to address the captain now that the medical procedure was finished. "Captain, Hoshi was able to get through to Starfleet, though all channels are on the fritz again now. But at least they know, and maybe someone'll even send help. We figure you were able to somehow discombobulate—"

"—the creature, yes," Archer finished for him. "Trip, you're not going to believe how simple it all is. It's a matter of—"

"Electricity," Trip said. "Simple electricity. Malcolm and I are putting together a device that generates an electrical field. We figure we can either zap Wanderer with it or somehow use it to contain the creature."

Archer stared at him. He was unsure whether to be glad or annoyed that Trip had figured things out before he, Archer, had a chance to save the day with his pronouncement.

Trip read his expression. "Well, it wasn't really *our* idea to begin with," he hedged. "Doctor Phlox was the one who suggested Wanderer might be feeding off the subtle electromagnetic fields we generate. That's why engineering flummoxes the creature. I didn't realize, but the warp engines generate a mild electromagnetic field, somewhat stronger than your average human body."

Archer nodded. "Good work. That's what incapacitated Wanderer, all right—probably at the very time Hoshi was able to get a clear channel. Now we just need to do it again—indefinitely, until we can figure out what to do with the creature. How long before the device is completed?"

"Not long at all. Thirty minutes, tops. We're just trying to be sure we can aim the darned thing so we don't electrocute ourselves. Speaking of which . . ." He looked pointedly at Archer's head; the captain lifted a hand to his hair and realized it still stood on end, then smoothed it as best he could. "Sounds like you had some up-close experience with our theory."

"Let's just say I had a personal encounter." Archer paused, then said, upbeat, "Get back to work, Commander. We need you to finish that thing."

Nearby, T'Pol listened to the conversation between the captain and Commander Tucker. She gathered that it could not be ascertained how much damage this electrical device might cause Wanderer—whether it would simply entrap the creature, or cause it great distress or damage, or even destroy it entirely.

Though she remained alert and standing, surrounded by other crew members, she permitted her mind to enter a waking meditative state, which she would end the instant required. Her instant of hesitation when Archer had ordered her to fire the pistol set on kill at Wanderer troubled her as much as her swiftness in firing at the Oani man who had attacked Hoshi—a fact she found perplexing, and so she sought to reason it out.

Had the kill setting actually disabled or destroyed Wanderer, then the *Enterprise* crew—and countless other humanoid races Wanderer might encounter in the future—would no longer be at risk. Was she, by refusing to take action against Wanderer, enabling murder?

The image of herself as a child, distressed over the dead *ch'kariya*, surfaced in her mind. She had known, even then, that the small, furry creature was no match for her in intelligence; its life was a dim shadow of hers in terms of knowledge and perception. Yet she had no right to deny it such a life.

At the same time, she realized that she fed on the death of plants, considered by Vulcans and all other humanoids to be nonsentient. Yet plants had sensation; they reproduced. They lived. How would she react if another, supposedly superior being called her a murderer because her physiology required her to live on them?

But they have been shown to possess no consciousness. Therein lies the difference.

How could she convince Wanderer that humanoids possessed a consciousness, when the entity could not detect it?

She thought of the Oanis, of the aesthetically pleasing civilization they had created, of their great love of peace—so great that they would harm not even a microbe. Certainly, Vulcan sensitivities did not extend that far; microscopic entities were attributed the same lack of consciousness as plants. The memory of those dead—of the Oani corpses, sitting patiently in the great hall of the medical facility—surfaced, and she considered for a moment what it would be like were the same catastrophe to befall her home, Vulcan. A great culture would be lost, one that was at present the greatest influence for peace on the known galaxy.

Wanderer certainly could not be allowed to take further lives. The question was in weighing the degree of force necessary to restrain the entity.

If the only way to do so was to destroy the creature—this unique, unimaginable being—could T'Pol justify doing so?

The question had particular relevance, since it was clear that someone was soon going to attempt to use the device against Wanderer. And T'Pol, since Wanderer felt ethically bound not to harm her, was the obvious choice. If she refused, she was possibly condemning one of her crewmates to death; if she agreed, she was possibly condemning to death a creature who had only peaceful intentions toward her.

She had promised herself, after killing the Vulcan-turned-smuggler Jossen, that she would never again be party to the death of another. But she knew she would need to make a choice soon, before the captain called upon her.

With Porthos in his lap, Archer permitted himself the luxury of sitting inside engineering and watching Tucker and Reed argue over exactly how the electrical device should be triggered. The relief from the agony in his shoulder now allowed him to realize the severity of his headache, and his level of physical exhaustion; even so, he was grateful that he and his crew had survived thus far . . . with the exception of Lieutenant Meir. He was still perplexed by the fact that she—or rather, Wanderer inhabiting her body—had left, and permitted him and T'Pol access to engineering.

But at the moment, he was too tired to try to understand. It was enough that Trip and Reed had a handle on the problem, and that for a moment he, Archer, got to sit down and pet his dog.

"No, that won't work," Trip Tucker was explaining calmly, with that intently focused look in his eye that Archer's dad used to describe as "the lights are all on and nobody's home." Malcolm Reed was listening, nodding, not taking the comment personally; the two were working together, getting it done. Archer smiled internally at the sight.

Abruptly, the lighting flickered.

Instinctively, Trip looked upward. "What the . . . ?"

The lights flickered again, then the entire room went utterly dark. Even the useless computer console at Archer's elbow flashed, then dimmed.

Archer sighed and rose, dog in his arms, as the murmuring began. "Everyone stay calm. Please remain silent so that I can direct you." Exhaustion kept his tone relaxed; inwardly, however, dread began to gnaw at him. In a flash, he understood exactly why Wanderer had chosen to ignore him and T'Pol, why the creature had considered it more important to use human hands and fingers to override more computer circuits. "Let's not go anywhere until we have to. If Wanderer's turned off life-support, the less we move and speak, the better." It occurred to him that perhaps he should put the dog outside, so that there would be more oxygen for his crew; but moving would only use up more oxygen, and the amount Porthos was using was minimal compared with a human.

He didn't admit to himself that doing so would also break his heart.

His people obeyed. For several moments, the room, which had before been filled with voices, was silent save for the low hum of the warp engines.

"Trip," he said. "You got any auxiliary lighting? I want you to keep working on that device, if you can."

"Yes, sir." Trip paused, and Archer could practically hear the engineer's mind working as he oriented himself in the darkness to the portable lamps he sought. The captain listened as Tucker made his way tentatively through the crowd to a cabinet, opened and closed it. An instant later, a dazzling beam from a flashlight cut through the blackness, throwing sharp, eerie shadows.

Archer said nothing as the two men worked in grim silence.

Minutes passed—at which point, the captain could no longer ignore that the room was growing cold and stuffy. Without life-support, the temperature would soon drop to subzero levels, and the oxygen would be used up by all the warm bodies.

"We're going to have to leave," Archer reluctantly told his crew. "Trip, Reed, you stay here as long as you can manage; try to get that device finished. The rest of you, follow me. We need to stay together."

He stepped through the doors of engineering—only to greet more crew members waiting in darkness. The corridor outside was equally chilly, and the air here was thinning as well. "We're sticking together," Archer told them. "Wait here."

He went back into engineering. "No life-support outside, either," he told Trip. "I can't risk you two being stuck up here and not having the oxygen to get to us. You're going to have to come, too."

Tucker scowled—not at the captain or his orders, Archer knew, but at Wanderer, for interrupting his work.

The captain handed Porthos—who had behaved remarkably well throughout the turmoil, as if sensing he should not add to his master's difficulties—to Hoshi. Taking Trip's flashlight, Archer led his people to the only source of light, heat, and air visible: the distant corridor beyond, leading aft to the main launch bays.

Wanderer was leading them down a path—one intended to culminate in their destruction, Archer realized, but at the moment he had no other choice.

In the first of the main-level launch bays, the lights were bright, the air fresh and comfortably warm. Archer stopped as his crew entered behind him, and spread out, filling the area around the shuttlepod. Hoshi moved next to him, in order to keep Porthos calm, and Reed and Trip Tucker came and sat on the deck beside them. Trip still held the electricity-generating device in his hands, and he and Reed bent over it, talking. They had opened up a phase pistol and replaced the internal mechanism with circuitry, to which some wiring was attached; Archer, weary but intrigued, sat down next to them.

Hoshi followed suit, and Porthos immediately went to his master . . . but couldn't help sniffing at the object Reed and Trip were showing such interest in.

"Easy, boy," Trip said. "You don't want to be getting a snootful of this."

Porthos sneezed in reply, then, obviously unimpressed by the mechanical object, went back and settled in Archer's lap.

"How much of a current does that thing have?"

"Not that much, in human terms," Reed said.

Trip clicked his tongue in contradiction. "Enough to curl *your* hair," he told the lieutenant, who instinctively ran a hand through his short, straight locks. "It won't kill a human," he said to Archer, "but it'll give 'em a jolt. We figure that if Wanderer can only handle a small amount of electromagnetism at a time, this ought to make it sizzle." He used a small needle-nosed pair of pliers to thread one of the wires to the weapon's trigger.

"Careful," Reed said, staring intently at the process. "Don't want to shock yourself."

Trip's upper lip curled slightly. "Now, that would take some talent, considering these pliers are insulated. I know a little bit about electricity, you know. We had some hellacious lightning storms down in the Keys. I knew when to come out of the water."

"Really?" Reed tried to imagine such a thing. "Do people ever actually get struck?"

"In Florida? You bet. People—tourists, mostly—get killed every year down there; at least, until the doctors revive 'em." Trip finally completed the circuit, set down his tool, and popped the cover back over the weapon, hiding all but the trigger. "Now all we've got to do is test her out."

"Forgive me if I don't volunteer," Archer said dryly. "I've had enough shocks for one day."

"Oh, she'll generate electricity," Trip said. "I'm just gonna aim her at the wall and make sure the beam goes where I want it." He rose and picked his way through the crowd—most of whom were now seated on the deck. A short distance from a bulkhead, he stopped, pointed the pistol, and fired.

A yellow-white beam streaked out from the business end of the pistol and struck the wall, crackling loudly for an instant before dissipating.

At the same instant, Trip gave a small yelp and dropped the phaser.

Reed stood and nodded skeptically while the

commander rubbed his offended hand. "Insulated, eh?"

Trip scowled at him. "I said the *pliers* were insulated." He glared down at the dropped pistol. "The trigger should be, too. I just need to . . ." He trailed off.

At the entry to the launch bay, Wanderer shimmered into being; the sight caused a hush to fall over those seated in the high-ceilinged bay.

The image of the dead Oanis, seated patiently in the medical center, flashed in Archer's consciousness. Despite his weariness, the sight of the creature filled him with rage. *It thinks it can just herd us here and pick us off, one by one.* He set Porthos aside and rose. "Hungry? Come on. Take me." He moved toward the creature, even as Hoshi followed and tugged at his arm. "Captain! No . . . !"

Archer firmly pushed her aside to safety.

"Step back, Captain!" Trip shouted. In one swift move, he crouched down, scooped up the dropped pistol, and fired it at Wanderer.

The effects—on both Tucker and the creature—were immediate. A bright bolt struck the entity, for an instant emblazoning its center with yellow sparks that turned swiftly green. Wanderer jerked upward in an eye-dazzling display of spinning cobalt blue and emerald—away from the crowd and Trip, who yelped again and dropped the pistol, flailing his hand.

The creature sailed straight to the ceiling, writhed there for a moment in a spasming pyrotechnic display, then vanished.

Archer ran to Trip, who was still flicking the wrist of the injured hand. "You okay?"

"I'm fine," Trip allowed, looking for an instant up at the ceiling, where the creature had disappeared. "Just a burn. But I dare say Wanderer'll think twice before it comes back."

Malcolm Reed appeared alongside the two men and picked up the dropped weapon. "Next time, Commander, all you need to do is take the cuff of your uniform . . ." He pulled his hand inside his sleeve, then tucked the fabric between the trigger and his finger. "See? It's very simple. It provides insulation. You needn't have shocked yourself."

Tucker graced him with a sour expression. "Yeah? Well, let's see how fast *you* think of insulation next time that creature comes back."

His last few words were almost entirely drowned out by Hoshi's exultant shout. "Captain! I've managed to get an open comm channel. We've received a message from Starfleet. . . . They've routed a Vulcan ship in our direction."

Archer felt a renewed surge of hope. "What's the ETA?"

"They didn't say, sir."

"Acknowledge receipt of the message, Ensign."

"Aye, sir."

Archer smiled at Trip and Reed. "Well, thanks to you two, all we have to do is wait until the cavalry gets here."

It was not, unfortunately, to prove that simple.

Hours later, in the vastness of the launch bay, T'Pol sat, cross-legged, her spine straight, eyes lightly closed. She was permitting herself to enter the first stages of meditation, though her mind would remain alert to all that was occurring around her.

It was evening again by the *Enterprise*'s Earth-based chronometers, and all about, the majority of crew members either leaned against the walls, lightly dozing, or curled up directly on the deck. Silence had fallen over the chamber, given that most of the personnel were exhausted. Even Captain Archer, who sat nearby in the company of Commander Tucker and Lieutenant Reed, their backs all supported by the nearest bulkhead, had fallen asleep, his chin dropped against his chest. In his lap, Porthos the beagle lay snoring, occasionally twitching as he dreamed.

T'Pol was aware that she had been spared a difficult decision concerning Wanderer: whether or not to help bring about the creature's demise. As it was, she was uncertain exactly how seriously the creature had been damaged by Commander Tucker's electrical pistol, but she fully expected Wanderer to recover and return.

And once the Vulcan ship arrived, that would not solve the dilemma of how to deal with the creature. No doubt enough electricity could be generated in order to destroy Wanderer—but T'Pol did not consider that a solution, and she doubted the other Vulcans would find it to be one, either.

Interestingly, her mind kept wanting to return to the long-ago incident with Jossen, and the lecture she had attended, listening to the *Kolinahr* adept Sklar on the question of self-defense and peace. T'Pol did not believe in intuition or the subconscious; Vulcan minds were trained so that all was conscious, and nothing buried; intuition was merely a human concept, for those whose mental machinations were so foggy that they were unaware that their "flashes" were the product of logical deduction.

Or so T'Pol had always thought. Yet an image kept returning to her: a centuries-old vid, restored from Old Earth newsreels, of a small, gaunt bespectacled human wrapped in a simple white cloth. *Gandhi-ji*, the people had adoringly called him. The elderly, frail man, all bones and dark flesh, had smiled at the crowds, who had thrown flowers and called him *Bapu*, Father.

She wondered whether the ancient Vulcans, with their passionate hearts and penchant for emotional display, had similarly welcomed Surak.

Somewhere, in the lesson of Gandhi, lay the solution for Wanderer. T'Pol's instinct knew this, even as her conscious mind rebelled. The notion had gnawed at her from the time of her earliest realization that Wanderer meant the human crew harm.

Were this so, I would be able to logically deduce why I believe this. Thus far, I have been unable to do so. Therefore, this line of thinking is irrational.

Yet the image of Gandhi persisted.

As T'Pol meditated, the doors to the bay hissed open.

She opened her eyes at once. In the entry stood Lieutenant Meir's reanimated body—possessed of an unnatural posture, the head listing with alarming limpness to one side—and in Meir's grip was a phase rifle. Meir's head and body swung about until they faced the captain and Commander Tucker, at which point she raised the phaser rifle and took aim at the electrical pistol, loosely held in the slumbering Tucker's hand.

T'Pol's keen vision detected that the rifle was set to kill.

"Commander!" the Vulcan shouted. She threw her body forward—enough to push against Tucker's thigh and startle him awake. Instinctively, he leapt up and raised the pistol in his hand.

Meir fired.

At the same time, Tucker dodged the killing beam as best he could and fired back.

The stream of electricity caught Meir full on, emblazoning her torso with a lightninglike display of dazzling blue-white. She twitched convulsively, dropped her weapon, and fell; like a wraith leaving her body, Wanderer emerged, again spasming as if in agony, then vanished once more.

At the same time, the rifle blast caught Tucker's hand; he cried out, sank to his knees, then dropped completely. The electrical gun dissolved in a brilliant burst, leaving behind the smell of molten metal.

Several things happened at once.

Captain Archer and Lieutenant Reed woke, and went to the aid of their friend, as did Dr. Phlox. The rest of the crew members woke as well, and the once-silent bay became a cacophony of sound.

"Trip, are you all right? My God, Doctor, hurry. . . ."

"Good lord, Commander. . . ."

"It's Meir! She's dead!"

Commander Tucker's groans added to the noise level. T'Pol took care to leave Dr. Phlox room to examine his patient, but she was close enough to see his wound in detail: The blast had completely burned away the tops of his three longest fingers to the distal joints. No doubt the electrical jolt he had received from firing the weapon had caused him to drop it immediately afterward—and Wanderer's aim had been perfect, intended not to kill potential food but simply to destroy the weapon.

Captain Archer's face, in profile, was deeply lined, a study in concern and suppressed fury as he knelt beside the wounded commander and asked Phlox, "What can you do for him?"

Phlox's expression, equally concerned, was also doubtful. "He's in shock. He needs pain medication badly, and antiseptic treatment for those burns. If I could get him to sickbay—or at least get him some medication . . ."

In reply, Archer himself went to the bay's double doors; they opened onto a darkened, airless corridor. He returned to Phlox's side and said, looking down at the still-groaning Tucker, "We're trapped. Wanderer's made sure we're not going anywhere."

"Dammit . . . all . . . to hell . . ." the commander swore between gritted teeth. "It killed . . . our device. . . ."

T'Pol wished, quite uselessly, that she could teach Commander Tucker the pain rules; however, it had taken her years of study to master them herself. She could hardly demonstrate to him how to relieve his own pain in a matter of minutes.

"The shuttlepod," Phlox said suddenly. "It has

an emergency medical kit on board." He hurried toward the craft.

Archer looked over at Lieutenant Reed, who was kneeling nearby with an expression of nauseated empathy. "Lieutenant. Do you think you could raid the shuttlepod for enough equipment to make another device?"

Reed looked uncertain, but he replied, "I can try, sir."

"Do it," Archer said. To Hoshi and T'Pol he said, "And in the meantime, let's raid it for water and rations. Wanderer's not the only one with an appetite around here."

Fortunately, Dr. Phlox was able to find pain medication for Commander Trip, and Ensign Sato took advantage of Wanderer's helplessness to once again open all communication channels. A message from a Vulcan vessel, the *Satar*, had been received stating that they anticipated arriving in eight-point-five hours; Sato replied in a recorded message, explaining Wanderer's nature and sensitivity to simple electricity.

In the interim, the *Enterprise* crew ate and drank, then once again fell into silence, waiting.

T'Pol could only postulate Wanderer's recovery time; however, she suspected that the type of electricity supplied by Commander Tucker's weapon was not the sort needed by the creature to survive. By this time, Wanderer would be hungry—

excessively so, if its previous feeding habits were any indication—and as soon as it was able, it would appear again, and pursue its prey aggressively.

She thought of the crowd of deceased Oani people who had been sitting cross-legged in the medical-facility waiting room. Perhaps they, too, had been herded there by Wanderer; perhaps they had awaited their death there patiently, unwilling to use any form of violence against the creature they had first thought their benefactor.

And once again, the image of Gandhi surfaced in her consciousness. Intrigued by its reappearance, T'Pol rose from her seated position and walked to where Lieutenant Reed sat leaning against a bulkhead. He worked with pliers and some pieces of circuitry pulled from the shuttlepod, but from the scowl on his face, she suspected he was making no progress on generating an electrical field. She sat back on her haunches beside him, and said, in a voice too low to wake those who slept nearby, "Lieutenant."

He glanced up at once, started to see that she was so close, then relaxed.

"Sub-Commander," he said, clearly surprised. "What can I do for you?"

"I hope I am not interrupting you at a critical time."

Reed let go a disgusted sigh as he gazed at the equipment in his hands. "It's critical, all right.

The fact is, what I need to make this work is over in engineering. Only I'll suffocate before I can get there; but if I don't try, Wanderer will kill us anyway. . . ." He looked up again, realized that she was still waiting, then added, "No, no. You're not interrupting me. Please. What did you need?"

The awkwardness of what she was about to do did not escape T'Pol; there was no other way to describe it except the human term, *making small talk.* Nor could she deny that what drove her to do so was suspiciously akin to intuition. "Lieutenant," she repeated. "You come from Great Britain. I assume you have heard of the twentieth-century leader Gandhi."

"Yes," Reed replied. "A truly great man." He paused. "Rather a pacifist, like your Surak. He followed the principle of *satyagraha,* passive resistance, to overcome injustices. What would you like to know about him?"

T'Pol hesitated. She had not known, until that precise instant, what she had intended to ask, but the words came to her at once. "I know that he used nonviolent protest to shame the British into surrendering control of India. . . ."

"Yes." Reed nodded. "I'm not proud of that part of my people's history. Thank God, they finally came to understand the injustice of imperialism."

"I would like to know specifically how the protests convinced the British to leave, even though no violence was used. Why did the protests shame them so?"

Reed's expression darkened. "In the beginning, the colonials—the Brits—thought all they had to do was fire their weapons into a crowd to disperse them. But the Indians wouldn't leave, wouldn't run. Not only that, when one of them fell, another would come to take his or her place. They simply wouldn't stop coming ... which would have forced the British into clearly immoral acts of gunning down innocent crowds."

A fresh image surfaced in T'Pol's mind, this time one of white-robed Indians, marching one by one against British soldiers, too many of them for all to be killed ... and then the image metamorphosed into that of white-robed Oanis, sitting cross-legged on the floor. Only these Oanis were not dead, but alive, their dark, luminous eyes open, and they sat with arms linked together. . . .

The solution, T'Pol realized, was simpler even than electricity.

She did not mean to be rude to Lieutenant Reed, but the critical nature of the situation demanded it. There would be time, later, to make apologies. She turned away from him abruptly, without excusing herself, and walked over to where Archer sat, dozing.

"*Captain,*" she said urgently.

* * *

Weak with hunger, Wanderer appeared again in the far corner of the shuttlebay nearest the airlock doors, by the ceiling, and swept gently downward toward the crowd like a sparkling blue-green tide rolling in to the shore.

There, on the deck, sat the *Enterprise* crew.

They sat in two large semicircles, cross-legged, pressed thigh-to-thigh, each one clasping the hand of two others; near the center of one half-circle, the wounded Commander Trip lay across the laps of his crewmates.

One of those crewmates was T'Pol; and as Wanderer approached, she called to it.

"You cannot feed on one of us alone. You must take us all together, or not at all."

In response, the creature neared until its periphery hovered just beyond the reach of the last person seated at the end of the first semicircle—Lieutenant Reed, who had volunteered for one of the end positions. He raised his face, sculpted hollows beneath his cheeks cast in shadow, and gazed up defiantly at Wanderer.

"We're conscious," he said. "Just like T'Pol. Just like you. We're not fodder to be eaten, and neither were the Oanis."

Wanderer hesitated for an instant—whether it did so because of what Reed said, T'Pol could not judge—and then, slowly, hesitantly, it moved toward the lieutenant.

The edge of the creature closest to Reed flowed

forth like an amoeba, engulfing the human's body. Reed shuddered, eyes snapping shut, jaw clamping, grip tightening on the hand of the crewwoman beside him. His body glowed from within, a phosphorescent blue-green. . . .

Eleven

AND THEN the phosphorescence traveled down the row of linked bodies, lightning-swift, fading as it sped across the semicircle until, as it reached the crewman on the other side, it dwindled to nothingness.

T'Pol, in the center of the crescent with Commander Tucker's head cradled in her lap, saw a flash of blue, felt the slightest surge of static electricity, and a mild dizziness that passed as quickly as it had come.

Abruptly, a transparent wisp of blue-violet ejected itself violently from Reed's solar plexus; the lieutenant gave a loud gasp, opened his eyes, and looked at the remnants of the creature in surprise.

Archer spoke up with authority, sitting beside

T'Pol with Tucker's torso across his knees; he held T'Pol's hand firmly in his cool human grip. "We never meant to hurt you," he told the creature. "You chose to try to hurt us—and T'Pol, whom you had said you would never harm." He turned to the Vulcan and asked, sotto voce, "Is it replying?"

T'Pol shook her head. "Negative, Captain." She was not sure that it could; she could not help wondering, however, what the creature was thinking.

In the launch bay, Archer stood in front of the open hatch of the shuttlepod and smiled faintly at Hoshi Sato as she walked toward him across the now empty-feeling chamber.

The Vulcan ship had departed several hours ago, with a special electrical chamber designed to contain the very weakened Wanderer; however, the Vulcan engineers assured the *Enterprise* captain that they would find a mechanical way to feed the creature. It would not be released until it could be educated and trusted to rely on its new form of nourishment, and not on humanoids.

Archer wondered whether that day would ever come—or whether, in fact, it *should* ever come. But he had been far too grateful to his Vulcan rescuers to argue the point; he was grateful, too, to have his ship back, and know his crew—and Earth—were safe. Trip Tucker's burned fingertips were currently being regenerated in sickbay, and Archer was free of his concussion and accompanying headache, thanks to Dr. Phlox.

Most of all, Archer was grateful for the experience of defeating Wanderer. It was more than the fact that the Oanis' deaths had been avenged, and that the *Enterprise* crew had been saved. The act of joining with his people against a common foe—and doing so in such a simple, meaningful way—had moved him.

It had not escaped his notice that T'Pol had instigated the linking of hands and touching of bodies together, or that she had later explained her reasoning for doing so as inspired by the passive resistance of an Earth leader, Gandhi. That she so unabashedly established physical contact with humans—an act Archer knew made Vulcans profoundly uncomfortable—and admitted to the fact that she had done so from intuition, *and* the example of a *human*, one that she actually admitted to respecting . . . *Well*, Archer thought, *wonders never cease.*

As for himself, he was beginning to rethink T'Pol's stance on refusing to carry a weapon. All the phase pistols in the world, as well as juryrigged devices, had ultimately proved useless against Wanderer. What *had* worked was the willingness of people to join together. Of course, that didn't mean Archer himself was willing to turn entirely pacifist; faced with a horde of Klingons, he'd be the first to reach for a pistol. But any anger he had nurtured against T'Pol for not wanting to bear arms had entirely evaporated.

If only the Oanis had known . . .

The Shikedans, at least, now knew the truth, as did the mysterious traveler who had met Wanderer, communicated with it, and been convinced by the energy creature that the Oanis were dying from a microbe. The Vulcans had contacted the Shikedans and made sure that all of them—including the traveler, who, contrary to Wanderer's insistence, had returned home to his people—were now aware of the danger the entity actually posed.

Hoshi finally reached Archer and paused at the pod's entry to show him the plaque she bore in her arms. It was of iridescent white shale, beamed up from the planet Oan, which they once again orbited.

"It's beautiful," Archer said. The soft stone had been allowed to remain in its irregular shape, but its surface had been polished, and beneath an alien inscription, the legend in English read:

In memory of the Oani people
Destroyed by the entity known as Wanderer
May their legacy of peace
Live on in the hearts of others

Hoshi smiled a brief, sad smile, then said, "That's in Oani script at the top." She paused.

"I've finished downloading their history into our databases. But I thought it'd be nice to leave a disk containing it at the memorial site as well."

"You've done a wonderful job, Lieutenant," Archer replied warmly.

As he spoke, Lieutenant Reed and T'Pol entered the launch bay within two seconds of each other—Reed first, who stepped aside and motioned for the Vulcan to pass in front of him. It did not escape his notice, or Archer's, that the sub-commander wore a phase pistol at her hip.

Archer gestured for Hoshi and Reed to enter the shuttlepod, then stared pointedly at T'Pol's pistol and gestured with his chin. Softly, he said, "What's this?" His tone was good-natured, but inquisitive; he had no desire, after all that had happened, to put her in an awkward situation.

She gave him a look of cerebral coolness; at the same time, he fancied he detected the faintest hint of good humor beneath it. "A phase pistol, sir."

Archer tsked at her. "I know that, Sub-Commander, I just . . ."

She dropped her pretense of literal-mindedness. "I have reconsidered my position on self-defense, sir. While I still feel the use of force should be avoided at all costs, there *are* situations where it may be necessary."

"Would it be too personal to ask what triggered the change? It seemed to me you did a pretty good job of showing what nonviolent resistance could achieve."

T'Pol paused. "The Oanis, Captain. Ensign Sato pointed out that they did not believe in destroying microbes. This made me reflect that it is possible to take a worthy concept to an unhealthy extreme." She glanced away no more than an instant, and it seemed to Archer that the faintest hint of reluctance came over her features. "It would not have been worth the destruction of their civilization. No more than it would have been worth allowing Wanderer to destroy human civilization, or any other group. It was mere chance that the creature could be defeated as simply as it was."

Archer nodded slowly. "I want you to know, T'Pol . . . that, whatever your choice is on this matter, I respect it."

"Thank you, sir."

Archer gestured toward the hatch. "Come on. Let's give the Oanis the memorial they deserve. I think you'll appreciate the monument Hoshi has designed."

She entered, followed by Archer; the hatch door closed, then the bay doors opened.

And the shuttlepod sailed once more toward the blue-green island planet.

Look for STAR TREK fiction from Pocket Books

Star Trek®

Enterprise: The First Adventure • Vonda N. McIntyre
Strangers From the Sky • Margaret Wander Bonanno
Final Frontier • Diane Carey
Spock's World • Diane Duane
The Lost Years • J.M. Dillard
Prime Directive • Judith and Garfield Reeves-Stevens
Probe • Margaret Wander Bonanno
Best Destiny • Diane Carey
Shadows on the Sun • Michael Jan Friedman
Sarek • A.C. Crispin
Federation • Judith and Garfield Reeves-Stevens
Vulcan's Forge • Josepha Sherman & Susan Shwartz
Mission to Horatius • Mack Reynolds
Vulcan's Heart • Josepha Sherman & Susan Shwartz
*The Eugenics Wars: The Rise and Fall of Khan Noonien Singh,
    Books One* and *Two* • Greg Cox
The Last Round-Up • Christie Golden
Novelizations
Star Trek: The Motion Picture • Gene Roddenberry
Star Trek II: The Wrath of Khan • Vonda N. McIntyre
Star Trek III: The Search for Spock • Vonda N. McIntyre
Star Trek IV: The Voyage Home • Vonda N. McIntyre
Star Trek V: The Final Frontier • J.M. Dillard
Star Trek VI: The Undiscovered Country • J.M. Dillard
Star Trek Generations • J.M. Dillard
Starfleet Academy • Diane Carey
Star Trek books by William Shatner with Judith and Garfield Reeves-Stevens
The Ashes of Eden
The Return
Avenger
Star Trek: Odyssey (contains *The Ashes of Eden, The Return,* and
    Avenger)
Spectre
Dark Victory
Preserver
Captain's Peril

#1 • *Star Trek: The Motion Picture* • Gene Roddenberry
#2 • *The Entropy Effect* • Vonda N. McIntyre
#3 • *The Klingon Gambit* • Robert E. Vardeman
#4 • *The Covenant of the Crown* • Howard Weinstein
#5 • *The Prometheus Design* • Sondra Marshak & Myrna Culbreath
#6 • *The Abode of Life* • Lee Correy

#7 • *Star Trek II: The Wrath of Khan* • Vonda N. McIntyre
#8 • *Black Fire* • Sonni Cooper
#9 • *Triangle* • Sondra Marshak & Myrna Culbreath
#10 • *Web of the Romulans* • M.S. Murdock
#11 • *Yesterday's Son* • A.C. Crispin
#12 • *Mutiny on the Enterprise* • Robert E. Vardeman
#13 • *The Wounded Sky* • Diane Duane
#14 • *The Trellisane Confrontation* • David Dvorkin
#15 • *Corona* • Greg Bear
#16 • *The Final Reflection* • John M. Ford
#17 • *Star Trek III: The Search for Spock* • Vonda N. McIntyre
#18 • *My Enemy, My Ally* • Diane Duane
#19 • *The Tears of the Singers* • Melinda Snodgrass
#20 • *The Vulcan Academy Murders* • Jean Lorrah
#21 • *Uhura's Song* • Janet Kagan
#22 • *Shadow Lord* • Laurence Yep
#23 • *Ishmael* • Barbara Hambly
#24 • *Killing Time* • Della Van Hise
#25 • *Dwellers in the Crucible* • Margaret Wander Bonanno
#26 • *Pawns and Symbols* • Majliss Larson
#27 • *Mindshadow* • J.M. Dillard
#28 • *Crisis on Centaurus* • Brad Ferguson
#29 • *Dreadnought!* • Diane Carey
#30 • *Demons* • J.M. Dillard
#31 • *Battlestations!* • Diane Carey
#32 • *Chain of Attack* • Gene DeWeese
#33 • *Deep Domain* • Howard Weinstein
#34 • *Dreams of the Raven* • Carmen Carter
#35 • *The Romulan Way* • Diane Duane & Peter Morwood
#36 • *How Much for Just the Planet?* • John M. Ford
#37 • *Bloodthirst* • J.M. Dillard
#38 • *The IDIC Epidemic* • Jean Lorrah
#39 • *Time for Yesterday* • A.C. Crispin
#40 • *Timetrap* • David Dvorkin
#41 • *The Three-Minute Universe* • Barbara Paul
#42 • *Memory Prime* • Judith and Garfield Reeves-Stevens
#43 • *The Final Nexus* • Gene DeWeese
#44 • *Vulcan's Glory* • D.C. Fontana
#45 • *Double, Double* • Michael Jan Friedman
#46 • *The Cry of the Onlies* • Judy Klass
#47 • *The Kobayashi Maru* • Julia Ecklar
#48 • *Rules of Engagement* • Peter Morwood
#49 • *The Pandora Principle* • Carolyn Clowes
#50 • *Doctor's Orders* • Diane Duane
#51 • *Enemy Unseen* • V.E. Mitchell
#52 • *Home Is the Hunter* • Dana Kramer-Rolls

#53 • *Ghost-Walker* • Barbara Hambly

#54 • *A Flag Full of Stars* • Brad Ferguson

#55 • *Renegade* • Gene DeWeese

#56 • *Legacy* • Michael Jan Friedman

#57 • *The Rift* • Peter David

#58 • *Faces of Fire* • Michael Jan Friedman

#59 • *The Disinherited* • Peter David, Michael Jan Friedman, Robert
    Greenberger

#60 • *Ice Trap* • L.A. Graf

#61 • *Sanctuary* • John Vornholt

#62 • *Death Count* • L.A. Graf

#63 • *Shell Game* • Melissa Crandall

#64 • *The Starship Trap* • Mel Gilden

#65 • *Windows on a Lost World* • V.E. Mitchell

#66 • *From the Depths* • Victor Milan

#67 • *The Great Starship Race* • Diane Carey

#68 • *Firestorm* • L.A. Graf

#69 • *The Patrian Transgression* • Simon Hawke

#70 • *Traitor Winds* • L.A. Graf

#71 • *Crossroad* • Barbara Hambly

#72 • *The Better Man* • Howard Weinstein

#73 • *Recovery* • J.M. Dillard

#74 • *The Fearful Summons* • Denny Martin Flinn

#75 • *First Frontier* • Diane Carey & Dr. James I. Kirkland

#76 • *The Captain's Daughter* • Peter David

#77 • *Twilight's End* • Jerry Oltion

#78 • *The Rings of Tautee* • Dean Wesley Smith & Kristine Kathryn Rusch

#79 • *Invasion!* #1: *First Strike* • Diane Carey

#80 • *The Joy Machine* • James Gunn

#81 • *Mudd in Your Eye* • Jerry Oltion

#82 • *Mind Meld* • John Vornholt

#83 • *Heart of the Sun* • Pamela Sargent & George Zebrowski

#84 • *Assignment: Eternity* • Greg Cox

#85-87 • *My Brother's Keeper* • Michael Jan Friedman

  #85 • *Republic*

  #86 • *Constitution*

  #87 • *Enterprise*

#88 • *Across the Universe* • Pamela Sargent & George Zebrowski

#89-94 • *New Earth*

  #89 • *Wagon Train to the Stars* • Diane Carey

  #90 • *Belle Terre* • Dean Wesley Smith with Diane Carey

  #91 • *Rough Trails* • L.A. Graf

  #92 • *The Flaming Arrow* • Kathy and Jerry Oltion

  #93 • *Thin Air* • Kristine Kathryn Rusch & Dean Wesley Smith

  #94 • *Challenger* • Diane Carey

#95-96 • *Rihannsu* • Diane Duane

    #95 • *Swordhunt*
    #96 • *Honor Blade*
#97 • *In the Name of Honor* • Dayton Ward

Star Trek®: The Original Series

The Janus Gate • L.A. Graf
    #1 • *Present Tense*
    #2 • *Future Imperfect*
    #3 • *Past Prologue*
Errand of Vengeance • Kevin Ryan
    #1 • *The Edge of the Sword*
    #2 • *Killing Blow*
    #3 • *River of Blood*

Star Trek: The Next Generation®

    Metamorphosis • Jean Lorrah
    Vendetta • Peter David
    Reunion • Michael Jan Friedman
    Imzadi • Peter David
    The Devil's Heart • Carmen Carter
    Dark Mirror • Diane Duane
    Q-Squared • Peter David
    Crossover • Michael Jan Friedman
    Kahless • Michael Jan Friedman
    Ship of the Line • Diane Carey
    The Best and the Brightest • Susan Wright
    Planet X • Michael Jan Friedman
    Imzadi II: Triangle • Peter David
    I, Q • John de Lancie & Peter David
    The Valiant • Michael Jan Friedman
    The Genesis Wave, Books One, Two, and *Three* • John Vornholt
    Immortal Coil • Jeffrey Lang
    A Hard Rain • Dean Wesley Smith
    The Battle of Betazed • Charlotte Douglas & Susan Kearney
Novelizations
    Encounter at Farpoint • David Gerrold
    Unification • Jeri Taylor
    Relics • Michael Jan Friedman
    Descent • Diane Carey
    All Good Things... • Michael Jan Friedman
    Star Trek: Klingon • Dean Wesley Smith & Kristine Kathryn Rusch
    Star Trek Generations • J.M. Dillard
    Star Trek: First Contact • J.M. Dillard

Star Trek: Insurrection • J.M. Dillard
Star Trek: Nemesis • J.M. Dillard

#1 • *Ghost Ship* • Diane Carey
#2 • *The Peacekeepers* • Gene DeWeese
#3 • *The Children of Hamlin* • Carmen Carter
#4 • *Survivors* • Jean Lorrah
#5 • *Strike Zone* • Peter David
#6 • *Power Hungry* • Howard Weinstein
#7 • *Masks* • John Vornholt
#8 • *The Captain's Honor* • David & Daniel Dvorkin
#9 • *A Call to Darkness* • Michael Jan Friedman
#10 • *A Rock and a Hard Place* • Peter David
#11 • *Gulliver's Fugitives* • Keith Sharee
#12 • *Doomsday World* • Carter, David, Friedman & Greenberger
#13 • *The Eyes of the Beholders* • A.C. Crispin
#14 • *Exiles* • Howard Weinstein
#15 • *Fortune's Light* • Michael Jan Friedman
#16 • *Contamination* • John Vornholt
#17 • *Boogeymen* • Mel Gilden
#18 • *Q-in-Law* • Peter David
#19 • *Perchance to Dream* • Howard Weinstein
#20 • *Spartacus* • T.L. Mancour
#21 • *Chains of Command* • W.A. McCay & E.L. Flood
#22 • *Imbalance* • V.E. Mitchell
#23 • *War Drums* • John Vornholt
#24 • *Nightshade* • Laurell K. Hamilton
#25 • *Grounded* • David Bischoff
#26 • *The Romulan Prize* • Simon Hawke
#27 • *Guises of the Mind* • Rebecca Neason
#28 • *Here There Be Dragons* • John Peel
#29 • *Sins of Commission* • Susan Wright
#30 • *Debtor's Planet* • W.R. Thompson
#31 • *Foreign Foes* • Dave Galanter & Greg Brodeur
#32 • *Requiem* • Michael Jan Friedman & Kevin Ryan
#33 • *Balance of Power* • Dafydd ab Hugh
#34 • *Blaze of Glory* • Simon Hawke
#35 • *The Romulan Stratagem* • Robert Greenberger
#36 • *Into the Nebula* • Gene DeWeese
#37 • *The Last Stand* • Brad Ferguson
#38 • *Dragon's Honor* • Kij Johnson & Greg Cox
#39 • *Rogue Saucer* • John Vornholt
#40 • *Possession* • J.M. Dillard & Kathleen O'Malley
#41 • *Invasion! #2: The Soldiers of Fear* • Dean Wesley Smith & Kristine Kathryn Rusch

#42 • *Infiltrator* • W.R. Thompson
#43 • *A Fury Scorned* • Pamela Sargent & George Zebrowski
#44 • *The Death of Princes* • John Peel
#45 • *Intellivore* • Diane Duane
#46 • *To Storm Heaven* • Esther Friesner
#47-49 • *The Q Continuum* • Greg Cox
    #47 • *Q-Space*
    #48 • *Q-Zone*
    #49 • *Q-Strike*
#50 • *Dyson Sphere* • Charles Pellegrino & George Zebrowski
#51-56 • *Double Helix*
    #51 • *Infection* • John Gregory Betancourt
    #52 • *Vectors* • Dean Wesley Smith & Kristine Kathryn Rusch
    #53 • *Red Sector* • Diane Carey
    #54 • *Quarantine* • John Vornholt
    #55 • *Double or Nothing* • Peter David
    #56 • *The First Virtue* • Michael Jan Friedman & Christie Golden
#57 • *The Forgotten War* • William R. Forstchen
#58-59 • *Gemworld* • John Vornholt
    #58 • *Gemworld #1*
    #59 • *Gemworld #2*
#60 • *Tooth and Claw* • Doranna Durgin
#61 • *Diplomatic Implausibility* • Keith R.A. DeCandido
#62-63 • *Maximum Warp* • Dave Galanter & Greg Brodeur
    #62 • *Dead Zone*
    #63 • *Forever Dark*

Star Trek: Deep Space Nine®

   Warped • K.W. Jeter
   Legends of the Ferengi • Ira Steven Behr & Robert Hewitt Wolfe
Novelizations
   Emissary • J.M. Dillard
   The Search • Diane Carey
   The Way of the Warrior • Diane Carey
   Star Trek: Klingon • Dean Wesley Smith & Kristine Kathryn Rusch
   Trials and Tribble-ations • Diane Carey
   Far Beyond the Stars • Steve Barnes
   What You Leave Behind • Diane Carey

#1 • *Emissary* • J.M. Dillard
#2 • *The Siege* • Peter David
#3 • *Bloodletter* • K.W. Jeter
#4 • *The Big Game* • Sandy Schofield
#5 • *Fallen Heroes* • Dafydd ab Hugh
#6 • *Betrayal* • Lois Tilton

#7 • *Warchild* • Esther Friesner

#8 • *Antimatter* • John Vornholt

#9 • *Proud Helios* • Melissa Scott

#10 • *Valhalla* • Nathan Archer

#11 • *Devil in the Sky* • Greg Cox & John Gregory Betancourt

#12 • *The Laertian Gamble* • Robert Sheckley

#13 • *Station Rage* • Diane Carey

#14 • *The Long Night* • Dean Wesley Smith & Kristine Kathryn Rusch

#15 • *Objective: Bajor* • John Peel

#16 • *Invasion! #3: Time's Enemy* • L.A. Graf

#17 • *The Heart of the Warrior* • John Gregory Betancourt

#18 • *Saratoga* • Michael Jan Friedman

#19 • *The Tempest* • Susan Wright

#20 • *Wrath of the Prophets* • David, Friedman & Greenberger

#21 • *Trial by Error* • Mark Garland

#22 • *Vengeance* • Dafydd ab Hugh

#23 • *The 34th Rule* • Armin Shimerman & David R. George III

#24-26 • *Rebels* • Dafydd ab Hugh

    #24 • *The Conquered*

    #25 • *The Courageous*

    #26 • *The Liberated*

Books set after the series

    The Lives of Dax • Marco Palmieri, ed.

    Millennium Omnibus • Judith and Garfield Reeves-Stevens

        #1 • *The Fall of Terok Nor*

        #2 • *The War of the Prophets*

        #3 • *Inferno*

    A Stitch in Time • Andrew J. Robinson

    Avatar, Book One • S.D. Perry

    Avatar, Book Two • S.D. Perry

    Section 31: Abyss • David Weddle & Jeffrey Lang

    Gateways #4: Demons of Air and Darkness • Keith R.A. DeCandido

    Gateways #7: What Lay Beyond: "Horn and Ivory" • Keith R.A. DeCandido

    Mission: Gamma

        #1 • *Twilight* • David R. George III

        #2 • *This Gray Spirit* • Heather Jarman

        #3 • *Cathedral* • Michael A. Martin & Andy Mangels

        #4 • *Lesser Evil* • Robert Simpson

Star Trek: Voyager®

    Mosaic • Jeri Taylor

    Pathways • Jeri Taylor

    Captain Proton: Defender of the Earth • D.W. "Prof" Smith

    The Nanotech War • Steven Piziks

Novelizations

 Caretaker • L.A. Graf
 Flashback • Diane Carey
 Day of Honor • Michael Jan Friedman
 Equinox • Diane Carey
 Endgame • Diane Carey & Christie Golden

#1 • *Caretaker* • L.A. Graf
#2 • *The Escape* • Dean Wesley Smith & Kristine Kathryn Rusch
#3 • *Ragnarok* • Nathan Archer
#4 • *Violations* • Susan Wright
#5 • *Incident at Arbuk* • John Gregory Betancourt
#6 • *The Murdered Sun* • Christie Golden
#7 • *Ghost of a Chance* • Mark A. Garland & Charles G. McGraw
#8 • *Cybersong* • S.N. Lewitt
#9 • *Invasion! #4: The Final Fury* • Dafydd ab Hugh
#10 • *Bless the Beasts* • Karen Haber
#11 • *The Garden* • Melissa Scott
#12 • *Chrysalis* • David Niall Wilson
#13 • *The Black Shore* • Greg Cox
#14 • *Marooned* • Christie Golden
#15 • *Echoes* • Dean Wesley Smith, Kristine Kathryn Rusch & Nina Kiriki Hoffman
#16 • *Seven of Nine* • Christie Golden
#17 • *Death of a Neutron Star* • Eric Kotani
#18 • *Battle Lines* • Dave Galanter & Greg Brodeur
#19-21 • *Dark Matters* • Christie Golden
 #19 • *Cloak and Dagger*
 #20 • *Ghost Dance*
 #21 • *Shadow of Heaven*

Enterprise®

Broken Bow • Diane Carey
Shockwave • Paul Ruditis
By the Book • Dean Wesley Smith & Kristine Kathryn Rusch
What Price Honor? • Dave Stern
Surak's Soul • J.M. Dillard

Star Trek®: New Frontier

New Frontier #1-4 Collector's Edition • Peter David
 #1 • *House of Cards*
 #2 • *Into the Void*
 #3 • *The Two-Front War*
 #4 • *End Game*

#5 • *Martyr* • Peter David

#6 • *Fire on High* • Peter David

The Captain's Table #5 • *Once Burned* • Peter David

Double Helix #5 • *Double or Nothing* • Peter David

#7 • *The Quiet Place* • Peter David

#8 • *Dark Allies* • Peter David

#9-11 • *Excalibur* • Peter David

  #9 • *Requiem*

  #10 • *Renaissance*

  #11 • *Restoration*

Gateways #6: *Cold Wars* • Peter David

Gateways #7: *What Lay Beyond*: "Death After Life" • Peter David

#12 • *Being Human* • Peter David

Star Trek®: Stargazer

The Valiant • Michael Jan Friedman

Double Helix #6: *The First Virtue* • Michael Jan Friedman and Christie
  Golden

Gauntlet • Michael Jan Friedman

Progenitor • Michael Jan Friedman

Star Trek®: Starfleet Corps of Engineers (eBooks)

Have Tech, Will Travel (paperback) • various

  #1 • *The Belly of the Beast* • Dean Wesley Smith

  #2 • *Fatal Error* • Keith R.A. DeCandido

  #3 • *Hard Crash* • Christie Golden

  #4 • *Interphase, Book One* • Dayton Ward & Kevin Dilmore

Miracle Workers (paperback) • various

  #5 • *Interphase, Book Two* • Dayton Ward & Kevin Dilmore

  #6 • *Cold Fusion* • Keith R.A. DeCandido

  #7 • *Invincible, Book One* • Keith R.A. DeCandido & David Mack

  #8 • *Invincible, Book Two* • Keith R.A. DeCandido & David Mack

  #9 • *The Riddled Post* • Aaron Rosenberg

  #10 • *Gateways Epilogue: Here There Be Monsters* • Keith
    R.A. DeCandido

  #11 • *Ambush* • Dave Galanter & Greg Brodeur

  #12 • *Some Assembly Required* • Scott Ciencin & Dan Jolley

  #13 • *No Surrender* • Jeff Mariotte

  #14 • *Caveat Emptor* • Ian Edginton

  #15 • *Past Life* • Robert Greenberger

  #16 • *Oaths* • Glenn Hauman

  #17 • *Foundations, Book One* • Dayton Ward & Kevin Dilmore

  #18 • *Foundations, Book Two* • Dayton Ward & Kevin Dilmore

  #19 • *Foundations, Book Three* • Dayton Ward & Kevin Dilmore

  #20 • *Enigma Ship* • J. Steven and Christina F. York

#21 • *War Stories, Book One* • Keith R.A. DeCandido
#22 • *War Stories, Book Two* • Keith R.A. DeCandido

Star Trek®: Invasion!

#1 • *First Strike* • Diane Carey
#2 • *The Soldiers of Fear* • Dean Wesley Smith & Kristine Kathryn Rusch
#3 • *Time's Enemy* • L.A. Graf
#4 • *The Final Fury* • Dafydd ab Hugh
Invasion! Omnibus • various

Star Trek®: Day of Honor

#1 • *Ancient Blood* • Diane Carey
#2 • *Armageddon Sky* • L.A. Graf
#3 • *Her Klingon Soul* • Michael Jan Friedman
#4 • *Treaty's Law* • Dean Wesley Smith & Kristine Kathryn Rusch
The Television Episode • Michael Jan Friedman
Day of Honor Omnibus • various

Star Trek®: The Captain's Table

#1 • *War Dragons* • L.A. Graf
#2 • *Dujonian's Hoard* • Michael Jan Friedman
#3 • *The Mist* • Dean Wesley Smith & Kristine Kathryn Rusch
#4 • *Fire Ship* • Diane Carey
#5 • *Once Burned* • Peter David
#6 • *Where Sea Meets Sky* • Jerry Oltion
The Captain's Table Omnibus • various

Star Trek®: The Dominion War

#1 • *Behind Enemy Lines* • John Vornholt
#2 • *Call to Arms...* • Diane Carey
#3 • *Tunnel Through the Stars* • John Vornholt
#4 • *...Sacrifice of Angels* • Diane Carey

Star Trek®: Section 31™

Rogue • Andy Mangels & Michael A. Martin
Shadow • Dean Wesley Smith & Kristine Kathryn Rusch
Cloak • S.D. Perry
Abyss • David Weddle & Jeffrey Lang

Star Trek®: Gateways

#1 • *One Small Step* • Susan Wright
#2 • *Chainmail* • Diane Carey

#3 • *Doors Into Chaos* • Robert Greenberger
#4 • *Demons of Air and Darkness* • Keith R.A. DeCandido
#5 • *No Man's Land* • Christie Golden
#6 • *Cold Wars* • Peter David
#7 • *What Lay Beyond* • various
Epilogue: Here There Be Monsters • Keith R.A. DeCandido

Star Trek®: The Badlands

#1 • Susan Wright
#2 • Susan Wright

Star Trek®: Dark Passions

#1 • Susan Wright
#2 • Susan Wright

Star Trek®: The Brave and the Bold

#1 • Keith R.A. DeCandido
#2 • Keith R.A. DeCandido

Star Trek® Omnibus Editions

Invasion! Omnibus • various
Day of Honor Omnibus • various
The Captain's Table Omnibus • various
Star Trek: Odyssey • William Shatner with Judith and Garfield Reeves-
     Stevens
Millennium Omnibus • Judith and Garfield Reeves-Stevens
Starfleet: Year One • Michael Jan Friedman

Other Star Trek® Fiction

Legends of the Ferengi • Ira Steven Behr & Robert Hewitt Wolfe
Strange New Worlds, vol. I, II, III, IV, and V • Dean Wesley Smith, ed.
Adventures in Time and Space • Mary P. Taylor, ed.
Captain Proton: Defender of the Earth • D.W. "Prof" Smith
New Worlds, New Civilizations • Michael Jan Friedman
The Lives of Dax • Marco Palmieri, ed.
The Klingon Hamlet • Wil'yam Shex'pir
Enterprise Logs • Carol Greenburg, ed.
Amazing Stories • various